MARY PARLOW
752-1875

# TUSCALOOSA

# TUSCALOOSA

*a novel*

## W. GLASGOW PHILLIPS

*W. Glasgow Phillips*

*William Morrow and Company, Inc. / New York*

Library of Congress Cataloging-in-Publication Data

Phillips, W. Glasgow, 1969–
     Tuscaloosa : a novel / by W. Glasgow Phillips.
          p.          cm.
     ISBN 0-688-12861-0
     1. Alabama—Fiction.   2. Family—Alabama—Fiction.
     I. Title.
PS2566.H528T87   1994
813'.54—dc20                                                      93–2481
                                                                      CIP

Printed in the United States of America

First Edition

1   2   3   4   5   6   7   8   9   10

BOOK DESIGN BY LINEY LI

FOR MY MOTHER AND FATHER

MANY THANKS TO MY EDITOR,
CHAS EDWARDS.

# AUTHOR'S NOTE

The events, individuals, and institutions in this book are fictitious. Any resemblance to real people or places is entirely coincidental. These characters are nothing at all like anyone I have ever met in Tuscaloosa or anywhere else. I love all the people I know in Tuscaloosa. I would especially like to say that the hospital in this story is nothing at all like Bryce Hospital, which has been taking excellent care of the disadvantaged for many years.

Experts and natives of Tuscaloosa will note that geography and history have been muddied slightly. Without describing an actual time and place, I have tried to capture the feeling of a certain area in the early 1970s.

**W.G.P.**

## chapter one

On the first night of their flight, on the third day of August in 1953, there was a hail of Old Testament proportions. Chunks of ice the size of shooter marbles pelted the car until my mother thought the glass might break, but as she and Carmen were on an errand of life and death and personal freedom, she stayed on the road. Carmen Rathberry was nervous, too; she fiddled with the dial on the radio, finally tuning in a gospel station from Mobile. They sang along with the hymns, which gave them odd comfort: odd, because they had just abandoned their families and were looking to get far enough away from us so that they could live a life of lesbian miscegenation in anonymity and relative peace. It was well known at the time that the Lord did not look favorably upon that kind of thing.

The hail beat on the roof in thrilling syncopations, Mardi Gras rhythms. They turned up the radio as loud as it would go, but the pounding of the hailstones on the steel roof made such a racket that they could only hear the joyful parts; the low, mournful parts were drowned out. It was as if they were inside the kettle of a mad drum major's instrument, which had hauled him at a sprint from the front of his parade, through back alleys, and into the swamp itself, where he ran on and on, foaming and crying out at the terrible joy of his possession, slicing his skin on the razored leaves of marsh grasses, bounding over the prostrate bodies of startled alligators. The drumming increased to a ferocious din, the sounds of percussion so close upon one another that they bled and echoed into a roaring orgy while the drummer's arms blurred in spastic inspiration; now the drumming slowed almost to silence, with each single hailstone breaking the stillness with an infinitesimally new tone, just when they thought the storm might have ended.

"It's like a regular plague, Carmen," my mother exclaimed, seeing how the grass lay flattened where the storm had passed, and the litter of ice on the asphalt.

"I reckon it is," said Carmen. "Looks like we're out from under it, though."

"Finally," agreed my mother, "finally out from under it," and they both laughed because my mother was speaking symbolically, the real regular plague being their husbands, life without one another, the pain of childbirth— I don't know, exactly. It makes me uncomfortable to concentrate on that, so I don't. How can you remember your mother's defection without some rancor? I admit that I feel some. I admit it.

But I do not blame her, nor am I angry at her memory. The manner of her reconstruction has made that possible. In fact, she has become a beacon for me. She is a distant flare in this murky twilight I find myself surrounded by so often. It is my hope that if I keep her in sight as I stagger around in the gloom, I may witness something that will make it possible for me to act myself. That is, for me to act at all. Because as it is right now, I am not good for much, though I am in the prime of my life.

It may seem a strange way to put it, to speak of "witnessing" an event for which I was not present, for which no one who can talk about it was really present. As for the ladies, they are dead. The Doctor may have been there, but he does not discuss the matter. Nigel knows no more than I do, and I believe his interest in the matter is worn out, anyhow. He has got concerns in the moment. Epiphany has been my main resource as far as factual details are concerned. She was not there, either, but she took it upon herself to place what she knew at my disposal when she deemed the time was right, which is to say when I asked, which is to say when I was ten and Nigel informed me that our mothers were roasting on spits in hell, and that if we were not good, we would have to eat them when we got there.

Epiphany gave me what facts there were as we snapped beans, in the same kitchen we sit in more than a decade later. They were really long beans, dusty green, as arched and muscular as springs. They are known locally as "snake beans."

I do not believe I evinced much surprise when she told me the story. Nothing seemed very strange to me at that age. People say that a child views the world with wonder, because everything is new. I believe that this is a myth; at least, it contradicts my experience. When I was a child, nothing seemed strange yet. It was all new and therefore all equally ordinary. I just filed the facts of my mother's death with all the rest: the taste of carrots, the smell of cut grass, how to clean a fish. It was not until much later that I found it necessary to make some sense of them. Not until just recently, until I found myself in a daze, overtaken by memories to which I have no claim.

They are memories of my mother, who is dead. I do not mean they were her own memories; in these memories I see her, and Carmen Rathberry, as if I were following them, or as if I were an unobserved guest. My father is also featured in these memories, and the surprise of it is that he is not exactly as I know him today. If I were to try to logically infer what his role was in the events, from the few facts that I have at my disposal, I would come to different conclusions than the ones that are being revealed to me in these visions.

All we really know, any of us (except for my father, the Doctor, that is) is that my mother and Carmen were lovers and fled and got burnt up in a fire. So the rest, it would appear, is imagined.

But I would have to disagree with that assessment. The truth is available. The truth can be divined from the scatter of dry bones. Looked at long enough, the bones will reveal the manner in which the meat once clung to them, and the meat will move in a fashion that can never be mistaken for anything but the truth.

So I proceed with what I remember. Like re-member.

Put back together. I remember it like this:

They were both a little blue after the hail, recalling the children they had left, but first things, after all, were first, and they were starting fresh. They held hands as they drove, and thought about burrowing their faces into each others' nooks and crannies.

So that is where I am when the girl comes around the corner from behind the house. I kick the beer at my feet over into the flower bed, where it foams forlornly, soaking into the loam. I am on the porch of my father's house, the last one on the right as you head down the drive toward the main building. Yellow coins of light that have fallen between the leaves of the live oak closest to the house slide crazily over me and the old boards of the porch, rushing from left to right in time with the rustling sway of the topmost branches.

I try to ignore the way I have punted my drink. She is lovely, with a terrible chopped haircut and no makeup and no shoes. She is flushed; strands of straw-colored hair stick to her forehead. She struggles with the zipper at the back of a yellow minidress, twisting like a contortionist with her elbows pointing all over the place and her clavicles in sharp relief over the wide neck of the dress.

"I can't get this fucking thing done," she says, squinting up at me and pointing over her shoulder at her back.

"Nothing worse than a sticky zipper," I say, motioning for her to turn around. It is true that I have a way with words. Women swoon. The zipper has caught on the fold of fabric that hides it from someone looking at the back of the dress. It is snagged pretty badly; I have to brace the palm of my left hand on the small of her back to get some leverage against my yanks.

"Ooh-la-la," she says while I am jerking her around.

"Oops," I say. It is an awkward couple of moments, but the zipper finally comes free, trailing a few yellow threads, and I slide it up to the base of her neck. The hairs there are blond and point inward and down the ridge of her spine. A light grease of perspiration makes them shine in the afternoon light. She steps away before I can get a good lungful of her smell.

"I appreciate that," she says.

"Shoot," I say, "it was my pleasure."

"I don't doubt it," she says. Her toes are curling into the black soil of the flower bed. A daffodil has met its happy end under the smudged curve of her foot. I tend those flowers, but I do not say anything. That daffodil is nothing to me right now.

"It got torn a little when I was getting the zipper loose," I say.

She laughs a big "Ha!" with her mouth wide open. She could give a damn. "It's not mine," she says.

"You borrowed it," I conclude, nodding.

"Right."

"Well, then. You can tell them it was my fault."

"I'll do that," she says.

"Won't you come up? And have a beer," I say.

"Why, thank you, I will come up. But some tea will be fine."

I make a motion over toward the stairs. It occurs to me

that she is probably some weird relative of one of the patients, maybe half-addled herself. She is seated in the second rocker when I come back out of the house, with a pitcher and two glasses.

"Do you like it sweet or unsweet?" I say. "Because this is sweet."

"Sweet is fine," she says.

"I think I will be switching to tea myself."

"It is a bit early for drinking," she whispers in a parody of primness. A herd of lunatics in smocks sports on the main lawn, under the supervision of a chunky nurse. It looks to be a game of duck-duck-goose. There are some unusual sights to be seen from these rockers.

"It looks like they're playing duck-duck-goose," I say.

"It sure does," she says. "It must do them a world of good to get out and play those wild games."

"Oh, they have a big time here," I say. This is not strictly true, all the time, but I know for a fact that there are worse places for the infirm to find themselves. "You must be here to visit one of your folks," I say, with a vague gesture that attempts to encompass the lawn in front of us, as well as the backyard and woods from which she mysteriously appeared.

"Why, yes, I am," she says. "I'm on an extended visit. What do you do here?"

"I am the custodian," I say. "The head groundsman, actually. I attend to the maintenance of the facilities here." I extend a hand. "I'm Billy Mitchell. Dr. Mitchell is my daddy. For the time being he is employing me here."

"I can see you are a real go-getter," she says.

"You bet," I say. "A go-getter is what I am when I am on

the clock. And in my free moments I sit on this porch until his stern gaze and general disapproval drive me to fishing."

She is courteous enough to show some teeth. "I'm pleased to meet you, Billy," she says. "My name is Virginia." Her hand is moist in mine, almost sticky, and the nails are bitten to angry red moons. She slips it under her thigh when she catches me looking at her fingers. They are pretty chewed up. She looks off at the ring of fools, pointing with her chin to draw my attention over there. The big old nurse is squinting in our direction, and we wave to her.

I experience a wave of proprietary fondness for the lunatics. I figure it must look to Virginia as though I am the plantation owner's son, surveying the expanse of my family's cattle and lands with a satisfied, benevolent eye. Then I realize that might not be such an attractive pose for me to be taking, in Virginia's eyes; it would make her cousin or brother or whatever one of my livestock. So I try to bleed some of the smug proprietorship from my expression, without sacrificing any of the benevolence. It is a fine line I am trying to walk with these subtle shifts of my facial muscles.

The nurse is craning her stout neck at us, obviously trying still to make out some detail that is just barely beyond her reach. She is counting off her lunatics but standing still; it looks to me as though she is explaining how to play to one of the patients who might have forgotten the nuances of the game.

"I'm afraid I have to be going," Virginia says, standing briskly. "Thanks for the tea."

"Oh, but you haven't finished," I say. The nurse is stomping toward us.

"You can have it," she says, and steps off the porch right back into the daffodils.

"Your shoes, though," I almost cry out. "Where are your shoes?"

"Billy, I have no idea," she says. She is walking away from me, away from the advancing form of the nurse, back around the side of the house toward the woods. Sure now, the nurse breaks into a trot and a full waddling sprint, hollering, "Damn you, Billy!" She holds her weird three-cornered hat to her skull in grim determination. I hear a whoop from the back-yard, and the nurse disappears in that direction. I follow to the edge of the porch and look around the house, in time to see Virginia take the fence in a track-star bound, dress up around her waist and white panties like a doe's flag over her strong legs. The nurse is clambering over, in hot pursuit, hopelessly outdistanced but undaunted, forging onward like a monstrous predatory goose. The herd of lunatics has joined me on the porch, milling and gabbling, and we watch the two women circling one another, bobbing and weaving brightly through the sparse pines, and listen to the ghostly peals of Virginia's laugh, spreading like bats into the sky.

It is later in the day, on toward the purpling hours of dusk, taking stealthy hits off a palmed joint in the long yard that backs up to the row of houses, that I come across her dis-carded hospital smock lying under an empty space in a clothesline.

The smell of the papermill hovers around Tuscaloosa like a secret fart in a hot room. It greases itself sadly along every sidewalk and pane of glass in the city, unless a breeze from the Gulf comes along to push it northward, and that happens less and less as the middle of summer approaches. Waking to it every warm, still day of their lives, people who live there forget about the smell of the papermill; the stink becomes subsumed into the torpid sadness and dread of drifting from one moment to the next, a constant minor note of dissatisfaction that plays on and on until it becomes inaudible. It is worst when the cloud ceiling hangs low and dark, before a rain, when the suspended moisture turns all the air into used breath, released and recycled in a vapor of damp tension and fear of suffocation. Townspeople, bug-eyed and short of breath, stagger doggedly about their business in ones and twos. If they are making conversation, it is hard to hear them at any distance. Sound falls flat and refuses to carry.

The note decrees that I am to meet my father in his office at the hour of eleven o'clock, which is fast approaching. Epiphany, all two-hundred Clorox-smelling pounds of her, sits at the table across from me. We drink black coffee, and I smoke and look at the comics. I have been able to do little else lately, besides mind the grounds. This project of recollection I have undertaken is causing a strange shift in my perception. All my dealings have become dreamier and dreamier, and the images on my inner screen, more and more real. It is as if they have finally resolved themselves to take some shape or other, after swirling foggily around one another for so long. I cannot divine what they are becoming, but I have a powerful feeling of their potential. I wait, and think, and feel that at any moment the design of things may present itself to me; its form will be as weighty and apparent as a prize tuber, I predict, but at this moment it is beyond my reach.

I may be mistaken, of course. It may be that I am merely drifting away, in the manner of a religious person. Religious people espouse the notion that the revealed truth is the only real truth. My experience with religious people is that they do not have a clear understanding of things. They are fucked up by what they variously perceive to be the revealed truth. I could be having a similar experience.

"What does he want me for?" I ask her.

"About a job," she says.

"I have a job, Fanny," I say.

"That's what I told him," she says.

Epiphany—"Fanny," of course, is the contracted form— has been my strongest ally ever since she told me the story of my mother's adventure with Carmen. She probably did not bargain for the fact that I would be a space cadet from then on out, but she has been good about it. I think it is rare that anyone knows what the consequences of anything will be.

"I hear you got a new friend," she says, moving her eyebrows up and down suggestively.

"Is that so," I say.

"That's so," she says. "It's the talk of the town that you've been courting one of the patients." I may not hear the end of my encounter on the porch for a while.

"Courting," I say.

"Un-hunh," she says. "Going steady with a lunatic."

"At least they're not in short supply," I say. "You might even be able to get one for yourself. They are not too particular."

"I guess not!" she says. "You're the proof!"

"Let's just keep this between the two of us," I say. "Daisy might get jealous."

"And she is sure worth holding on to, boy," says Fanny. "That one's going to be right cute when she de-butts." Daisy Brehard, who I guess is my girl, is broad in the beam, and she is to be presented to Tuscaloosa's polite society in the coming year.

"It's getting a little warm in this kitchen," I say.

"If you can't take the heat, get on out," she says. "The Doctor is waiting."

"Maybe I'll just finish my coffee," I say.

"All right," she says. "Hand me that front page."

I face the occasion of a meeting with my father with some trepidation. I do not feel entirely at ease with him.

I have only known my father, of course, in the time after my mother's flight. It is my understanding that he was changed by the events that transpired in those few days. It would be an exaggeration to say that he was broken by them; rather, I would say that he was bent. Until that time he had never considered the possibility of defeat.

His father was a dirt farmer, and he was being raised to be a dirt farmer, but I guess he did not like the look of his future and decided to make something of himself. His primary and secondary education were undertaken in a one-room schoolhouse out in the country near Peterson. There was the usual business of walking nine miles, even in the winter, to get there every day, and the work in the fields in addition; during planting and harvest he skipped two schooldays each week to help Papa. It was the Depression; times were hard. At seventeen he took a bus to Tuscaloosa with a blanket and six dollars and slept in a ditch for the week it took him to make the first string on the Alabama football team. In that week he ate nothing but hot dogs bought from a cart in the parking lot, and at the end of it he was given a full scholarship for his four undergraduate years. After that he attended the medical school at the university. By that time he was presentable enough to meet and become engaged to my mother, who was from a fine old family that had been broken down by the Depression.

They were married, and happily so, it seemed, from all reports. He was a vital man, a legendary athlete, and an excellent psychiatrist. In seven years (during one of which he was not even in Tuscaloosa, but in Guam), he became the director of the largest mental hospital in the South. My mother was a beauty and an intellectual. Though I suspect that everyone believes these two things of his mother, in my case I am fairly certain they were true. A few photographs and the memories of others attest to the former. As for the latter, the only fruit of her scholarship that remains is a slim volume of poetry that was published by the university press; it was well received in academic circles. Though we do not keep a copy in the house, I went to the library and read it once, at a sitting, from cover to cover. It dealt largely with birds of prey wheeling over rocky promontories, and I am afraid it went mainly over my head. In addition to her beauty and her intellect, she had the makings for being a fine wife in the manner of fine wives at the time; her family had been broke long enough that she had become practical.

The Doctor is not a hard man to like; he is handsome and funny. There were no obvious reasons that she would be unhappy with him, though I guess it is possible that he had been running around on her. On the other hand, maybe she and Carmen had been in love for years before they left; that is the simplest and most lovely explanation. It could have begun when he was in Guam, fixing holes in the minds and bodies of American wounded. No one ever suspected, least of all the Doctor. It was the only event in his life, as far as I have been able to trace it, that surprised him. I secretly believe that he has never recovered, though you would never know it to look at him. He still appears, to most, as tough and shrewd and sure as a boar, but I think he is in pain. The reason I believe this is that on occasion, in our private moments, I have a flash of feeling of deep relation to him that would be impossible if he were not also damaged.

Because my father does not see himself as damaged, this feeling causes me discomfort. It is the feeling of trying to hand a palsied man a cup of tea; you know he will shiver the cup from its perch on the saucer, but he holds out expectant hands—what are you to do? Only, the feeling is infinitely more subtle than that, as there is not another in the world who would agree with me in my analysis of the Doctor. He has encysted his own view of himself into the persona he has erected for public viewing. No one, not even I, has ever seen him actually shake.

The hot breath of July blasts wetly into my face as I step outside, onto the porch. My shirt is beginning to stick before I get to the steps, and in only a few strides my feet become slippery in my Weejuns. It is a good thing that I have purchased some mirrored sunglasses; they block out most of the sun's inimical glare and render me inscrutable. I have been trying to become inscrutable for some time, especially when dealing with the Doctor. I am trying to nurture the illusion he may have that we no longer understand one another, though in fact I believe I am just beginning to see him clearly.

His dog, Marmalade, is squared off at the head of the broad steps to the front door of the hospital. The hospital is something to see, if you are used to thinking of a hospital as a low, flat, modern building with tall windows that cannot open and floors of linoleum and very short pile carpeting, or as a formidable building in a city, fed by screaming ambulances. Branson is nothing like that at all. In fact, you might not even know it was a hospital if you saw it for the first time without noticing the sign out front, or noticing that there are a lot of people wearing green and white all over the place, and some hints of institutional decor: white lines for parking places painted on the asphalt in the drive, chair after wicker chair lined up on the veranda, too many for a family and too stiffly arranged for entertaining, all staring dumbly out from behind the tall fluted columns at the lawn and live oaks of the approach. In its sprawling grace and inviting white- and greenness, the hospital resembles an old plantation.

Marmalade does a shuffle step as I approach. She is fond of me, as I have never done her wrong. Her dam had the misfortune to have been our dog during the years of my childhood and early adolescence and never eyed me without a trace of suspicion and dim memory of abuse. With a show of devotion I bend down to pat Marmalade's head. It has become a point of pride with me that this dog actually likes me, though I feel indifferent toward her. She is too much of a simperer for my taste, but I do not think she sees through my charade of affection. What people say about dogs' instinctive ability to know goodness is nonsense. Marmalade has a brain somewhere between the size of a marble and the size of a walnut. I do not know exactly, only that it is quite small. The Doctor probably knows exactly.

Dogs will like you if you are good to them, regardless of whether you are a good person; it is a pleasure to me to have Marmalade's affection, even if I know it is not the simple thing she believes it to be, but the product of my own greedy, backhanded servility toward her. We part with beaming eyes as I open the wide screen door, and then the big white wooden one, and step in. The screen door slaps to with a startling bang. After the bright heat of the outdoors, it is dark in the entry hall, and cool as a sepulchre. The central air-conditioning is hard at work with a solid, believable hum. The varnished benches that border the room are empty. The receptionist's desk is unmanned, and I slide on by.

The Doctor's office is at the far end of the entry hall. To the uninitiated, the first few steps into Branson might be a little bit eerie. Behind the motorized purr of the air conditioners and fans there is a constant human murmur. Voices, not quite intelligible, rise and fall in a gentle babble from distant reaches of the old building. There is the feeling of a great many people somewhere just out of sight, lurking perhaps around the next corner or behind the closed door to your left. But this is an aural illusion, created by the strange acoustics of the high ceilings and long breezeways of the building. In truth, there is nothing creepy about the hospital, as long as you are not frightened by the insane themselves; and they are not as dangerous, or as strange, as they are made out to be. They are only people who have gone ever so slightly wrong; I am often confounded when I consider how narrow is the range of behavior that is considered sane. The insane are brought here to heal if healing is possible, and to live out their days if it is not. The hospital is as well run and modern as any facility in the entire South.

There are still some peculiarities about the management of the institution, some ways of going about things that are left over from earlier days, before there were such strict rules about state-administered health care, but nothing that would spark your curiosity. The main thing is that the Doctor manages the hospital practically single-handedly, with care and casual efficiency. Patients and doctors alike revere him. He has given over a good portion of his life to the hospital, and it is his word that is the law in there. For an insane asylum Branson is a remarkably calm and pleasant place. He calls to me from behind the door to his office, which is slightly ajar.

"Boy," he calls out, "is that you?"

"Yessir," I reply, stepping in. I do my best to project respect and alertness, but I can hardly see a thing from behind the mirrored sunglasses. He is a bulky shape silhouetted by the window.

"What in the shit have you got on your face, Son?" he asks me.

"Sunglasses, Dad," I say.

"Look like a damn Martian," he says. "It's as dark as a tomb in here, anyway." He motions for me to take them off. I place them in my breast pocket. "Have a seat," he says. I sit in a leather-cushioned chair facing the cluttered expanse of his desk. There is a basket of ripe, dusty peaches on his desk that color the whole room with their heady smell. Motes of dust swim in the column of light that falls over the Doctor's shoulder onto the peaches. He leans back, resting the base of his ass on the windowsill, and places his meaty palms on his knees. It is like an umpire's half-crouch: casually meditative and aloof, but invested with unquestionable authority. He does not practice these movements. They come naturally to him. The Doctor is a man who commands attention and respect and affection without intending to, almost against his will. He is prone to winking greasily at receptionists and cashiers younger than I am. And in the most serious of conversations he is likely to cough up a huge oyster of phlegm and snot and amble over to the garbage can and spit into its bottom with a resounding metallic thump, all the while keeping his eyes on the speaker. But these movements have a grace about them that belies their banality. I think I am something of a disappointment to him because I do not have the same grace. It is not that people do not find me likable. They do. I am simply not remarkable. I am a very ordinary person. I think that is probably what I have been summoned to explain.

"Lawn's looking good," says my father. There is a hint of sarcasm in his tone: not to say that the lawn is not looking good, but to question whether lawn maintenance is worthy of the attention I give it. I nod. "I been down to see Mr. Brehard," he continues. "Man says he has got an opening."

Mr. Brehard, Daisy's father, is the owner and publisher of the newspaper downtown. He is not a bad man. He is one of my father's cronies. In high school I did some layout for him, and corrected spelling and grammar on the occasional letter to the editor. I delivered papers when I was in grammar school. He and my father are of the opinion that I have a literary bent. This is not so. The fact is that I spend a good deal of time reading. I do not have too much interest in anything else to do with books, or newspapers. It continues to surprise me how difficult it is for people, my father particularly, to believe this: that you can be absorbed by something and not want to participate in it. Besides, Mr. Brehard's newspaper is hardly the place a person would go to exercise a literary bent. Tuscaloosa may be the center of certain things, but it is no cultural Mecca, and the columns on the editorial page of Mr. Brehard's paper tend to be about Bear Bryant, or the First Breath of Spring, or, when one of the writers is struck by a fit of political fury, the Colored Problem or Our Boys in the Far East.

But I am not one to protest vociferously. "Cool," I say.

"I am glad that you find it so," says the Doctor. "Mr. Brehard suggested to me that if you were interested, you might make an appointment to visit him downtown some time in the next week or so. When you can find the time."

"Dad, as you know, I am a busy man," I say. "In the summer the grass grows very quickly. But I think I can find the time to visit Mr. Brehard very soon. I will make it a priority."

And so, in the Doctor's eyes, the matter is settled. The interview with Mr. Brehard is a mere formality. There is room for me on his staff. But I do not want to go to work for Mr. Brehard. It would mean that I would spend less time on the grounds, and I do not want to forsake my work among the shrubs for a job in an office. And besides, if I were working downtown, my father would probably try to get me to rent an apartment there and move out of my room in the house. That, too, would be a great inconvenience. I find that my imaginative memory flows most freely here, and then there is Virginia. I would like to run into her again. What excuses could I use to get back to Branson as often as I wanted to? Filial devotion is only believable to a point, especially in a relationship so cordial and distant as the one between myself and the Doctor. After all, I went to college at the university, which is practically contiguous to Branson, and rarely made it over to the hospital. These are things to think about.

"Do you want a peach?" asks the Doctor.

"They smell crazy," I reply, breathing in over them and poking one gently with my forefinger. "And they're huge."

"Biggest damn peaches I ever seen," he corroborates, selecting one from the top of the pile. He has it halved and pitted in no time, slipping his penknife around the longitudinal circumference of the fruit with customary assurance, and prying the dimpled pit from the bright flesh with a flick of the knife's tip, into the wastebasket at his feet. The two halves lie in his palm like tennis balls before a serve.

For me every moment is loaded. This is the curious moment in which I see that but for the darkening and thickening of age, his hands are my own. He eats his half over the wastebasket so that the juice that escapes his mouth drops neatly into it, and then wipes his fingers with a handkerchief from his back pocket. As I eat, I try to keep the juice from spilling over into my palm, but it is impossible. The peach is too ripe; juice runs down my forearm toward my elbow. There is a brown spot in my half of the peach that I failed to notice when I took it from my father's hand. It has been bruised and gone sweetly rotten. I swallow it without mention.

It has often been noted that the sense of smell is particularly joined to memory, and to whatever murky caverns in the mind contain the sexual and imaginative faculties. So it is no surprise to me that when I bring the discarded smock to my nose and breathe in its various scents, I am able to recreate for myself that scene in the flower bed. Virginia has left the smell of herself caught between the nap of the faded cotton material and the sanitary odor of detergent.

I find that if I breathe too deeply or rapidly, I lose the smell of her in the stronger scents with which it has become entangled. I fold the smock into a loose ball and take in its odors in short, intermittent breaths. The smell I am looking for is no perfume, but the tangy stink of her sweat and some heady, feral musk that unfolds behind my closed eyelids into the contours of her figure.

Slight of bone but sturdily muscled, she leans back in the rocker with her bare feet square against the boards of the porch. The damp of perspiration beads on the skin of her neck and shoulders and the valley leading down between her small, childish breasts, and she hitches the yellow of her skirt above her knees, where the muscles and tendons of her legs move in a shadowy rhythm with her rocking, and she parts her thighs slightly to allow entrance to what breeze blows in across the lawn. She balances the glass of tea on the arm of the rocker, and the light clink of the concussion of swirling ice cubes against the glass comes to me with the creak of the old rocker rolling on the boards. She brings the glass up to her pale, cracked lips and pulls deeply, and the slow peristalsis of her throat and the quiet gasp of satiation after freeze me in my own rocker, and she turns to me with her eyes, her eyes that though wide almost seem hooded in epicanthic folds, that though clear might best be described as the color of babyshit, a strangely limpid muddy green, and that is the end of it.

Morning light breaks across the front acreage. The early shadows of the oaks slice the lawn into fresh strips, which steam softly as the day warms. Walking across the grass is like walking on a cool tongue.

Latham is waiting for me at the toolshed. As always, he is wearing his green-and-yellow John Deere baseball cap. It rides way up high on his head; when you look at him in profile, you can see right through the mesh in the back half of the cap, over the top of his scalp. He squats with his back to the corrugated tin and sips coffee from a thermos cup. Without fail, he is here before me. If I am early enough, I might get to share a joint with him and have a cup of coffee myself. Today I am too late to get high, but on time for some joe. I fetch an enameled mug from the toolshed and blow the curled carcass of a spider from its bottom. Latham's coffee is rich and foamy with cream and sugar. We sip gingerly, as it is hot, and balance on our haunches.

"Madcap mayhem day," he comments.

"Yeah," I say. "I'll take care of it."

"Okay then," he says. "I'll go down and see if that paint come in at the store."

"Great," I say. "Good plan."

"All right then," he says. He pours himself another inch of coffee without changing his position. His shoulders hunch toward his ears, and his forearms rest on his knees. His long-fingered hands hang comfortably at the wrist. He is still a good squatter, for such an old man. I am trying to accustom my thighs to the long periods of squatting that accompany con-versation with Latham. My grandfather is also a fine squatter. I believe it comes from working in fields, where there are no chairs when you need to rest. You develop your squat out there, when you are young, and it does not leave you.

"All right then," he says again, and stands. He gets the keys to the truck from the hook inside the toolshed and heads on over to where it is parked. It grinds up, and he putts away.

Latham's position is a strange one. I am officially the head groundsman, but that is a position created especially for me; it did not exist until I graduated from college last May and was right there to fill it. That is nepotism for you. In actuality, Latham has been the head groundsman longer than I have been alive. He worked for my grandfather out on the farm until Papa quit running it and moved into a trailer; then Latham came to work for the Doctor at the hospital.

Though I have been running around on the grounds my entire life, it is not unreasonable to say that Latham is more of an expert on how to keep the place looking right. He has got experience and the proverbial green thumb. Our dialogues constitute a weird charade of real and pretended authority.

"We had better do some pruning on those elms out back," I might say.

"Mm-hmm," he might respond, "them azaleas are fixing to get choked dead."

"We'd better get to those azaleas, I guess," I might say.

"You right about that, Billy," he might say. If I ask him straight out what we should do next, he just looks off watery and shrugs as if he has got no idea.

Latham is also a participant in the larger charade of courtesy that constitutes the manner in which we all deal with one another. Latham dislikes my father, though I believe he likes me well enough, and I know he gets on with my grandfather. But the thing is this: that Latham and the Doctor cannot give voice to their inimical feelings. To do so would violate a central tenet of the agreement we have all silently signed. In our personal dealings we are courteous to a fault. We would do anything. But I have seen the sunspots on the Doctor's car after Latham gets through waxing it. And I know it gave the Doctor some small degree of satisfaction to put me in a position of authority, however ridiculous, over Latham, though the Doctor is the first to give lip service to Latham's invaluability. His ability to praise is the measure of his power.

"Old boy keeps it looking good, don't he?" says the Doctor, flicking the butt of a smoke off into the lawn, where it sends up a thin blue signal. "Ain't a man around knows as much about horticulture." The linen of his coat sets off his tan and blue eyes in just the right way.

The Doctor has a harder time dealing with Latham's grandson. Nigel has chosen to divorce himself from the charade. He is a year younger than I am. I remember the two of us climbing around on the Doctor's back in the front yard. Caesar, Nigel's father, was working at his church, or maybe traveling; Nigel was spending the day in Latham's custody. The Doctor was a cow, and we were wolves; we jumped all over him growling and snapping, and the Doctor turned in a most uncowlike fashion and bit Nigel on the leg. Nigel has since defined his own position. The Doctor believes that Nigel is a subversive element. He has got an Afro the size of a beach ball. You do not see too many of them in Tuscaloosa; growing an Afro tends to preclude certain kinds of employment. But Nigel works at Paradise. They are an equal-opportunity employer.

The reason for the tension that hangs between Latham and my father and Nigel and myself is simple. Latham's last name is Rathberry. He is the father-in-law of Carmen Rathberry, my mother's lover, who burnt up with my mother in an oil fire over a freeway in Texas in 1953, when I was three years old. Carmen was Nigel's mother; she was also our maid. Caesar Rathberry married Carmen (then Carmen Jacobs) a year or so before my mother and the Doctor tied the knot; Carmen's family had worked for my mother's for time out of mind (or rather, for as far back as it is polite to remember), so it seemed a pleasant coincidence when my mother married the Doctor. I imagine it made things convenient for a while, and later on I imagine it made for some uncomfortably close quarters.

The vehicle was not identified for some days, and the bodies were burned so completely that there was no trace of them; that is what Fanny told me. It seems that they drove past the first part of the fire, not realizing its extent, and when they tried to return, they found their way blocked by the flames.

Our living and working in such close proximity to one another after the event would probably seem strange to someone from somewhere else. At times it seems strange to me; if we are sources of pain to one another, if we are reminders to one another of things that shame us, why don't we all simply turn away and go our own ways?

Perhaps in other locales it is that simple. But to us, that was not an alternative. The adults put the matter aside as if it had never happened and went on. As for Nigel and me, what were we to do? We grew up in the shadow of a huge, invisible tree. Even today we are not sure where its branches grow; we cast about for their locations by feeling for the cold pockets in the air, and by means of that blind, two-dimensional mapping, we try to extrapolate its height, its girth, the million twists in its limbs.

I root around in the toolshed until I unearth the box of equipment I need, and walk back toward the rear of the main building. My work on the grounds is a source of great pleasure to me, and I reflect again, with distaste, on the fact that I will be expected to leave it.

It is not that I am unwilling to apply myself. In fact, I do. Under Latham's oblique guidance, I manage the grounds of the hospital with efficiency, commitment, and some measure of sweat. Latham considers that for a white boy, I am a hard worker.

Though I am no hippie, I believe there may be some truth to the hippie credo that enlightenment waits in a return to the soil. I find that my work provides a physical backdrop appropriate to my emotional needs, and an entrance into the state of recollection. Each day is a return to former shapes; each day is an attempt to rediscover primary forms.

I cannot expect my father to understand how pleasant I find it to mind the grounds. Or maybe that is not quite it: He understands that I find it pleasant, but it is not in him to find real satisfaction in such an endeavor. He can enjoy mowing the grass only if it is an orderly prelude to great thought and activity to come, or perhaps as a respite from those. Mowing is no end to my father. To him the constant return to the same form, with maintenance, rather than progress, as the goal, would be a Sisyphean hell. But that is him. He is a great believer in progress, while I am not.

Three days a week, legions of lunatics are at my command.

We clip, we mow. Together we cut back the lush greenery of the grounds to meet the careful contours of cement at each curb and sidewalk and building's edge. We impose the geometry of stone upon the wild, careless spawning and growth of the hedges and lawns. There are no decisions to be made; the shape each shrub is to take was determined long ago; it is ours merely to slough and carve away the detritus and new growth until we come to the perfect, regular polygonal shape locked within. The labor pleases me, in its order and repetition, and I find that it is an excellent preparation for my evening visits to the cranial cinema.

The Doctor's practice of using his patients as yard help may seem unconventional, but it is actually a tradition left over from the first days of the hospital. When the hospital was established, it was at the center of a working farm, and the patients supported themselves on the land. There are no longer any crops, of course; the government makes sure everyone is fed. But the patients still help take care of their home away from home. I believe it is called "outdoor therapy" now. The truth is that this activity is far from inhumane. They love to do it; it is regarded by most as a privilege and a sign of health, because the more severely afflicted patients cannot participate.

My ragtag crew is milling about at the foot of the back stairs of the hospital. They wear the motley colors of the lunatic gardener: gloves and work boots in addition to the customary green pajamas. I distribute hedge-clippers from the box. They are the kind that fit in one hand, with curving handles covered in orange plastic. Using tools of this nature with my crew of gardeners gives me some pause, but they are by and large a docile lot. And if, by chance, one of them should become angered and attack himself or another with the clippers, it would have to be a digit-by-digit dismemberment; no limb of greater girth than a thumb's can fit into the small jaws of the orange clippers.

We turn to the hedge of privet that encircles the main building of Branson. This will be a week's project; my crew's attention span is such that we can only work for two hours a day. That is enough time to give them some exercise and fresh air and a feeling of having accomplished something.

The bright new growth falls away without incident under our patient assault; it is slow going with the small clippers, which can only sever one shoot at a time, but we are in no hurry. Occasionally I step back a few paces and study the pleasing difference between the squared, even contours of the clipped hedge and the disorderly furriness of the hedge that has not yet been clipped. I follow a few feet behind the rest, catching spots they have missed, raking the clippings into piles that I will collect, with Latham, after my crew has returned to the cool and quiet of card games and television in the long halls and lounge rooms of the hospital.

The reason Latham is at the paint store instead of with me right now is that he has pretty much abdicated his responsibilities as a lunatic manager. Dealing with the patients has never been his favorite part of the job; several times there have been squabbles, and I remember that once he turned a hose on his entire crew and sent them bawling and scattered to the four winds. I think it is partly because of his distaste for dealing with the afflicted that Latham exhibited no resentment at my being installed as head groundsman. Essentially, he has been provided with an assistant who has no more than titular command over the operation of the hospital plant; now he has got someone who will deal with the foolishness of the work crews. And I am happy to work for Latham, within the bizarrely coded structure of authority we have erected. I believe Latham has silently accepted my silent apology, but as we are both silent about it, I will never know for certain.

The forward shrubbery scouts run into a beehive during my reverie. There is panic, and much braying and disorder. It is a rout. My ability to keep order has been entirely undermined by this unexpected encounter. I find bee stings as unpleasant as the next person and keep myself at a reasonable distance from what seems to be the center of activity. The ones who flip around the most fare the worst.

I quiet my fool gardeners as best I can, and take stock of the casualties. They are not so bad as they might have been; only four people have actually been stung, and of those, only one received more than one sting. He is a pale, larval boy, who looks as though he were a project not quite brought to completion. There are two stings on his right arm, and one on the back of his neck. They are swelling into angry pink boils, white at the center. The two of us watch with mounting concern as they fill with some hot, horrible humor. I imagine that he is in great pain, but he is a stoic. Or perhaps he lives at a great distance from his sensations.

The Doctor once told me how a patient put a finger through the grate of a powerful wall fan and chopped his finger into pieces like the coins of carrot that you might find in a salad. When someone came upon him and asked him what he had done, he put another finger through the grate before they could stop him, and chopped it to pieces, too. There has since been a protective grating of finer mesh put over the face of the fan.

🍑

"You going to dream yourself to death, boy," he says.

The glass nestled in the crotch of my pants has gone wet with condensation, and the last warm sip is pale and thinned with melted ice. It tastes like spit. The Doctor stands in front of me with his putter and a bucket of balls, which he tosses one by one out onto the lawn.

The grass directly in front of the house is a special hybrid from Scotland that the Doctor ordered for the purpose of seeding his own putting green. The seeding of the kidney-shaped green was one of the few occasions when the Doctor supervised hospital maintenance personally; he sat on the porch and directed Latham and me as we stripped up the old grass, turned the dirt below, and scattered the seeds. The resultant turf has a surprising, spongy texture. If you kneel and examine it closely, you can see that it looks more like a lichen or moss than grass. The blades grow in kinky spirals, weaving themselves into a tangled carpet, which appears almost synthetic in texture when it is closely mowed. From time to time the Doctor comes out with his highball and stomps around on the grass wearing a pair of sandals shod with roofing nails. The nails extend a good two inches below the soles of the sandals, which are big enough to fit right over his regular shoes. According to the Doctor, the nails allow air to penetrate to the roots of the strange grass, which cannot survive unventilated. The shoes also come from Scotland; apparently the people there take their putting seriously.

"Aeration, boy," he says as he tromps.

This time he is in his regular golf shoes, white ones with a rakish fringe over the laces. He roams from ball to ball, tapping them cleanly into the regulation hole that Latham and I set into the green. He varies his style for the balls that have fallen close to the hole, putting from behind his back, between his legs, or looking off into the middle distance.

"You got to live in the world, Son," he says to me. I have not moved from my post in the rocker.

"I know," I say. "It is just that I have got this lethargy. I need to think some things over, too. I have been feeling powerfully strange."

"Lethargy, you say."

"Yessir."

"This ain't just another ploy to get some Benzedrine," he says.

"No," I say.

"Hell, I had what you got," he says. "Nobody wants to think that his days at Bama are done."

"That must be it," I say.

"You just getting started," he says, executing a ballerina's twirl into a backhanded putt. The ball disappears with an annoying click onto its conquered brothers in the pit.

He scoops the balls out one by one with the hook of his putter and taps them all away from the hole again. He knocks one pretty hard in my direction; it bounces through the geraniums and hits the porch with a resounding clunk. I perk up a bit. He aims his club at me like a dueller with a dragoon pistol. "All you need is to get off your ass, boy. You need some work that will involve your head," he says, not unkindly. "All this moping is bound to mess you up."

"I am not unhappy," I say. "I'm just taking some time, that's all."

"Shit," he says, "you feel like going to Europe or some such place?"

"No thanks," I say, "but I appreciate it."

"That's fine," he says, as if something has been settled. He squats, sights toward the hole, and knocks one in croquet-style, with the blunt nub at the rear of his putter head. The ball goes wide of the hole and sits quietly a foot beyond it. He has followed its failed arc with his eye. He forgets me; he sucks his dental bridge sadly and shakes his head.

It is a wonder to me that a man whose profession is the management and rehabilitation of the mentally ill can have no inner life; that is the appearance the Doctor gives most of the time. You would think that association with the insane might lead to self-examination. That has been the case with me. But perhaps the Doctor is able to maintain a more clinical perspective; surely it is not fear that keeps him from peering into the darker halls and parlors of his heart, where recollection and reconstruction are undertaken.

A peppermint-blue Buick purrs up and parks itself in the driveway, which is a reminder to me that my father's plans for me are not the only obstacle to my achieving a life of simple work and reflection. There is also Daisy Brehard, the daughter of my former and possibly future employer. The matter of Daisy Brehard has been causing me some niggling discomfort; it is a situation illustrative of the type of waffling and weakness to which I am prone.

"Hey y'all," she hollers out the window. She is a blur of accessories: sunglasses being propped from eyes to forehead, lipstick applied while we watch her and then tossed to melt down on the passenger seat, silk scarf adjusted over coif, cigarette extinguished. She steps from the vehicle as if from behind a curtain, presenting herself with a palms-up, hip-cocked pose.

"Hi, Daisy," we chorus.

"Well, isn't that the cutest," she exclaims. "Miniature golf."

"Just working on my stroke so I can take your Daddy's money," says the Doctor, slapping in another. She is taken by a fit of giggles.

"You are too much, Dr. Mitchell," she says. I mumble about cold drinks and go in to get some beers. Fanny is bent over looking in the fridge, and I poke her in the butt. She roars and kicks back at me like a mule.

"You better watch it, smart boy," she says. "I can still whip you with one hand." It is probably true. If that kick had landed, it would have hyperextended my knee.

"Daisy's here," I tell her.

"Did you break the news?"

"The news?"

"You know, the news, lover boy," she says.

I get down into a boxing crouch, and wave her in with

curling fingers. "Come on and get some," I say. She bats my left down and wrings my nipple about off. She lets go when I squeak. I go over and look into the fridge, keeping a wary eye over my shoulder.

"Ain't no more cold beers in there," she says. "Look back in the pantry." Fanny fills three tumblers with ice cubes and refills the trays, and I take a six-pack and the glasses back out front, with a pause in the hall for breath and consideration.

The truth is that I am more or less betrothed to Daisy. Or at least that is how I fear that she sees it. I have not made any objections to her proclamations of ardor; in fact, I am willing to concede that at first I may even have encouraged them and uttered some words of affection of my own. She is, to tell the truth, in possession of my fraternity pin: no great matter, perhaps, but in these parts no small matter either. Pinning her seemed at one point to be the path of least resistance, in those days of confused eye contact and unspoken misunderstanding after she first gave herself up to me (and she was my first, too, though I never did tell her) in a horrible, messy, quiet tangle on the seventh fairway of the Indian Hills Country Club. Tuscaloosa is no exception to the tendency toward a vestigial puritanism that characterizes our region, and I must admit that I have not been altogether able, by sheer effort of will, to rid myself of the instinct toward chivalric guilt that is one of its components. I cannot muster the surge of courage that would be necessary to make a clean break with Daisy, and our relationship seems to sail sedately onward, unaffected by my passivity. It is my hope that my utter lack of ambition will drive her away. That is one of the reasons that I have made no secret of my post as a yardman. But I fear that my sloth will not be sufficient to discourage Daisy.

I do not mean to sound as though I am great shakes as a catch. Clearly, I am not. It is just that Daisy lives in an unquestioning manner, and I doubt that she has ever applied her scrutiny to the tangled web of obligation that has wrapped itself around us, or ever considered the possibility that either one of us might want to extricate ourselves from it. If one of us has any reason to be dissatisfied, it is Daisy, but I have got the feeling that it has never occurred to her to wonder whether she is satisfied with me.

She is attractive after a fashion, in that rounded, sunny way that sorority women tend toward, which is the evidence of three family-style meals a day: a tendency toward matronly fatness already showing itself in the dainty bulge above the brassiere strap, where it curves past the shoulder blade and under the arm, or in the slight dimpling on a seated thigh before the shorts are primly pulled down. But it is a Venusian plumpness, suggestive of comfort and jollity; there is nothing fallen about it. And Daisy is a sexual creature. That first time on the grass may have been grim, but since then we have become accustomed to one another's embrace, and she has even taken—I do not know where Daisy heard of these heathen pleasures, but I have to say that it pleases me to no end—to taking me into her hot, minty mouth. So every time I see her, bouncing confidently toward me, or rolling up the drive made up and smelling right in the cool blue interior of the Buick Skylark her daddy gave her, I am unable to come any closer to the truth, in speech: that I am not in love. Not with Daisy.

And I think that Daisy is probably not in love with me,

either. I think she is in love with what she perceives to be my potential, and she is doomed to disappointment if her plans for union ever come to fruition. Daisy tells me she has a feeling she just cannot shake that I will make something of myself. This is a grave miscalculation.

When I step back out onto the porch, Daisy is standing in a putter's pose, my father's club gripped loosely in her fingers. He stands behind her, hands over hers, illustrating the proper swing.

"Your daddy's teaching me to putt right!" she exclaims happily. Behind her, he smiles wanly and looks off into the trees. I set the glasses in my hand on the porch rail, and jack the tops off three lukewarm beers. The ice jumps and pops as the foamy amber liquid breaks over it.

I become absorbed in the details of my work. The process of unearthing several yards of the pipe leading to sprinkler heads along the back of the main building has taken the better part of an hour and put me into a sweaty stupor. When I hear a rapping on the window just above me, I jerk my head up in surprise and bang it on the overhanging planter.

"What?" I yell, not recognizing the smear of face that appears behind the grid of wire and glass. The window creaks open a crack, and half of Virginia's face appears, resting sideways on the sill.

"Billy!" she hisses in a stage whisper, with a big show of rolling eyes and stealth.

"Virginia," I say, whispering, "what?"

"What are you doing?" she asks.

"Planting geraniums," I lie.

"You have to rescue me," she says.

"Why?" I ask.

"Because I'm not crazy, you dumb shit," she says.

*c h a p t e r   t w o*

They started to get tired in the wee hours of that first night. They took turns driving to relieve the exhaustion of moving without rest. When it was her turn to rest, my mother laid her head in Carmen's lap. Carmen's calloused fingers played with great promise through my mother's curls.

She imagined that Carmen's fingers were travelers returned after a long journey in a savage land, where they had often longed for home. The fingers walked all over her head, tracing her scalp, drawing the curves of her ear. They caressed the short hairs of her eyebrows and dipped into the hot of her mouth. Grateful for having arrived back safely, they took their time, certain of repeated returns and a reestablishment of the familiarity they had once known.

Carmen and my mother ate fruit out of an icy cooler whenever they were hungry or thirsty. When they ran out just after dawn, they stopped and bought more from a desiccated old farmer seated beside his pickup on the highway. He had his fruit spread out on a peeling card table, and a coffee tin for a till. They pretty much had their pick of what kind of fruit they wanted, as long as it was peaches. They ate so many peaches that Carmen said they might be shitting cobbler by nightfall.

"I don't care what I shit, as long as I don't shit it in Tuscaloosa," said my mother. The discussion of shit was liberating to both of them, and the image of cobbler, steaming, sweet, and shiny, streaming out of one another's assholes, erotic in the extreme. They found that the fabric of their inhibitions was unraveling at the exact rate of their flight. Mile by mile, it spun out behind them. They felt the effects of its unraveling physically, in a loosening of their muscles, surprising pops in their spines, surges of blood through capillaries that had lain for years in brackish stagnation. My mother's face went hot. A curious pounding began in her womb, and her vagina contracted spasmodically, flooding her lap.

"Carmen!" she gasped, clawing at herself in astonishment, but Carmen had her eyes shut and her hands on the dashboard, and was quaking in the throes of an orgasm no less staggering. They were beginning to find that the journey they had undertaken was to be even stranger than they had anticipated.

What was it about, exactly? That was a question that my mother, Anne Mitchell, asked herself as the last warmth faded from her face and throat, and her breath came naturally again. What were they running from, and what were they running to?

"That was something!" she said to Carmen.

"Yes," said Carmen, "it was."

"It makes me wonder," said Anne.

"Wonder if there is not more to this, even more than we thought," completed Carmen.

"Yes," said Anne. There was a new day opening in the rear window. It had caught up to them and had them on its breakfast plate.

"It's a spiritual thing," said Carmen.

"Well, yes, it may be," said Anne, "though it is embarrassing to refer to it as such." She smiled, shyly, to indicate that she did not mean to criticize; on the contrary, she understood the difficulty of verbalizing such matters.

"I am renouncing sin," said Carmen. "It does not suit me."

"Renouncing it?" asked Anne.

"Not quitting it," said Carmen, "but just leaving it behind."

"I think we may be beyond the bounds of sin, that's what I think," said Anne.

"Maybe that's it," said Carmen. "Maybe we don't even need to renounce it."

"I feel as if it never had anything to do with me," said Anne.

"That's it," said Carmen. "That's what I'm saying." She picked up another peach and blew some road dust off it. The peaches had gotten dusty growing in that orchard next to the highway. She took a big wet slurp out of it. "I just can't get sick of these things," she said.

"Nothing like summer peaches," said Anne.

"Nope, nothing," said Carmen. She looked over at my mother, where she sat behind the wheel, on the other side

of the fruit. Carmen asked Anne to take fruit and break it
on herself.

"Take this one," she said, selecting a peach that was
absolutely perfect, "and this one," she said, finding another
even fatter and riper. Smiling, Anne drove with a peach in
each hand, steering with the pale bellies of her wrists.

"Now just dig into them, and let them run all over
you," said Carmen. Anne dug in lightly, with her sensibly
short nails, and the juice began to run. "Yeah, like that, but
more," said Carmen, and Anne did it, blushing a little bit at
first, but then squeezing down as hard as she wanted, and
pressing the broken flesh to her throat, her shoulders, her
breast. "That looks like it feels good," said Carmen.

"It does," said Anne.

"Now in your lap, and eat some at the same time," said
Carmen. Anne held fruit to every part of herself that she
could reach, and broke it there and rubbed the flesh against
her own, and Carmen pointed, saying, "There," and,
"There." No matter where she pointed, there was no
conjunction of Anne and fruit that made either one of
them ashamed. The whole thing just made them happy.
They did not feel bad about wasting all that fruit, and they
were not afraid that anyone was watching.

About the only time the lot fills up at Branson is during visiting hours. Generally I sit on the porch of our house with a bottle and imagine family histories as the cars roll in. It is good enough entertainment. When I was a kid, it took something like a bucket full of frogs to drop off an embankment into traffic to keep me entertained, but dreamier pleasures satisfy me now. The frogs at Harrison pond are in no danger from me anymore. They go about their business.

There is no telling what kind of car is going to roll up, or what manner of bizarre occupants are going to be mooning out its windows. Affliction has no bias. It will as soon attach itself to the rich as to the poor, to the black as to the white. You might see a gleaming Lincoln drifting in, with a driver in front and a blue-haired old lady sitting up like a statue in back, the whole rig cleaner than heirloom china except for the film of bugs on the bumper that it picked up on the way down from Charleston. And behind it will be a pickup truck with the cab popping with six wall-eyed, towheaded crackers, come to visit the child in whom backwoods genetics finally went completely wrong: a skinny kid with translucent skin and DNA full of tangled recessive near-impossibilities. Once, a hunchbacked crone the color of ash, who could not have been four feet tall, came in on a wagon behind a balding mule, and once a whole school bus full of Baptists arrived unannounced to spread the Word among the afflicted. Needless to say, I have myself a good time, usually. It is better than the Bama synchronized swimming team, and under normal circumstances I would make myself comfortable and check it out. But that is not the case today. I have got other tripe to fry.

Foo Foo is minding the desk. Her name is only one of the unfortunate things about Foo Foo. I believe it is a contraction of Fiona, but that is no more than a hazarded guess. Reading a novel by an African writer recently, I came across the word "foofoo." It was some kind of yam dish, which I imagined to resemble sweet-potato pie, in Nigeria. But I doubt that Foo Foo has been exposing herself to the latest in African literature, or that she would name herself after a yam dish even if she has. It has also occurred to me that "foofoo" might have been her first word, an infantile attempt to get her lips and tongue around the word "food," but that is an uncharitable thought. She is what in local parlance would be termed a biggun.

"Foo Foo, how you making out?" I say.

"I just been out to Paradise," she says. "I'm fixin' to melt." This may be true. There is a runny aspect to her face. She is glazed, like a ham, in a solution of sweat and makeup, which is setting up in the comparative cool of the office. She fans herself with a doughy white hand and bats gummy eyelashes at me. I flatter myself with the thought that Foo Foo has got herself a wet spot for me, and give her a simpering smirk of my own. This is one of the times I am glad that nobody follows me around with a movie camera. If I had to see my idiocy played back for me anywhere but in the empty rooms of memory, I would go crazy myself.

I take my place at the end of a seated line of relatives and friends of patients. It is kind of a weird scene, up close. Some of them make me nervous and sad. There is an old man next to me, sitting on the edge of his chair. His wattled neck sticks straight out from the empty arch of his seersucker coat collar, parallel to the floor, and his chin almost comes to rest on the folded knobs of his fingers, which are wrapped around the head of his cane. I figure this may be his last Sunday visit to a sick wife, or daughter.

"Billy," Foo Foo trills over at me, "you can just go right on in and see your daddy."

"You can wait your damn turn like the rest of us," the old man snarls at me.

"Yessir," I say. "Hey, that's okay, Foo Foo."

"Mister," she says to him, "that there is Dr. Mitchell's son," causing the gazes of all assembled to turn upon me.

"You think I give a god damn, you heifer bitch?" he hoots. Foo Foo gasps. This is an unfortunate scene, I think. I had hoped to keep a lower profile.

"Foo Foo, no," I say.

"Why, yes indeed," she says. "And there is no call for that kind of talk."

"It's your turn," I say to the old man.

"You damn right," he says. "I drove damn near an hour and a half, all the way from Birmingham, and I be a god damn if some little peckerwood snot going to skip on in front of me."

"Yessir," I say. "No doubt about that." I wink over at Foo Foo, as if to say, "Foo Foo, let us have this be a little private joke between us. There is no need to take this old feller seriously." That may seem like a lot of message to cram into one wink, but if you think about it, it is not so much. Winks have borne more. But Foo Foo is having none of it.

"Now you listen here, mister," she says.

"Foo Foo," I say.

"And you simmer down, too, you," she says to me. I think the heifer bitch part is what has got her going, and my lack of response to it. But there I am, pinned between my obligations to femininity and venerability. I have the conciliatory yearnings of the born diplomat, but my tongue is of no service. "Mister," she says, "this here boy is just going to see his daddy, who works here. His going in there is not going to slow you up one little bit."

"Foo Foo," I say, "but that's the thing."

She interrupts her monstrous schoolmarm finger-wagging and puts her arms akimbo. Biceps and triceps settle slowly into place, like a car dieseling after the engine is cut off. The families are watching.

"Exactly what is the thing?" she says.

"I'm not here to see my daddy," I say.

"I see," she says. "Well, whatever you're doing, go on and get about it."

"But that's the thing," I say. "I'm here on a visit."

"To whom?" she asks.

"God damn," says the old man. "I been in the car for damn near two hour."

"That's right," I say. "It's not my turn."

"Damn," he says.

"Damn," I say. There may be an understanding brewing between us. I slip him the same wink I tried to slip Foo Foo a while back.

"That hippo is an ear short of a bushel," he whispers to me. "You go on ahead."

"Her name's Virgina," I say, to Foo Foo.

"Virginia what," says Foo Foo.

"I don't know," I say.

"Damn," says the old man.

It is a good five minutes before Foo Foo figures out which patient I am looking for, and finds her file, and sends somebody up to get her. I feel like a bug in a jar by the time Virginia pads down the stairs. The waiting families have been watching my colors change. There is an air of expectation in that waiting room.

The waiting room was designed much like the entry hall in a mansion, pared down to its essentials; a curling staircase winds down into one side of it. At visits, the patients descend by means of that staircase to see their families, which lends an odd formality to the occasion; the staircase foregrounds the role of the visitors as such, and puts the patients, in terms of spatial relations, in the position of hosts, rather than prisoners. I cannot imagine that the architect intended this, but it is an interesting effect. It makes me feel like a guest who has been told by the maid, "Wait here."

Virginia stands at the top of the stair like a demented belle in pajamas. I wave to her from the bench. She comes on down, and the journey is eternal. It is one of those situations in which you are not sure how far away the other person should be before the first verbal communication is initiated. She is right there in the same room, but far enough away, on the staircase, that I would have to raise my voice for it to reach her. I wait until she has made it to the floor, and say "hi." I extend a hand, which she shakes seriously.

"This is what you call a rescue?" she says to me.

"I thought we should get to know each other before we run off," I say.

The standard visit on a clement day usually consists of walking around on the front acres. The patients and their families form little clumps that wander aimlessly, making sure only that they do not come too close to one another. It looks like a dozen suspicious Hebrew shepherds grazing their little flocks of twentieth-century civilians, making sure that they don't mingle. There is no way I can hike around out there, especially after that weird scene in the waiting room. We go out to the porch.

"Do you like to fish?" I ask.

"Sure," she says.

"Tell you what," I say. "I'll go get my car, and we'll go get us a mess of bluegill."

"Hot damn," she says.

"Then it's settled," I say, taking her by the elbow, heading toward the house.

"I know the way," she says, but she does not pull her arm away.

"Uh, right," I say, remembering.

"I trust that lady got her dress back okay?" she asks.

"Ah, Miz Cutrell," I say. "Yes, she did. I believe it was fine after she sent it to the cleaners'."

"It was a nice one," says Virginia.

"It became you, I mean, looked good," I say. "You appear to be in pretty good shape."

"I ran the four-forty before I quit school," she says.

"Well, that explains it," I say. We are at the open mouth of the garage.

"Nice car," she says. "That's a road-trip car."

"Thanks," I say.

She is telling no lie. It is a lovely car. I run my hand along the front fender. It is one of the longest front fenders on any production automobile. I drive a white convertible Eldorado which is run down but not short on style. There are some rust spots along the right side, where the trim peeled off against a telephone pole placed injudiciously close to the roadside; the top leaks when it rains hard. But when the vinyl rolls back and eight fat cylinders of Detroit steel go to pounding, you quit caring you are in central Alabama.

I take the fishing poles from where they lean against the garage wall and toss them into the backseat. I point to a pair of the Doctor's overalls that hang on a hook. "Put those on if you want," I say. "You can change inside." She puts them on right there, using her smock as a changing room. I am charmed by this show of feminine dexterity. Though our visit is going well so far, I decide that it is prudent to establish a few things before we set out.

"Now, Virginia," I say, "you are not going to throw a fit out there or anything, are you?"

"Not me," she says.

"Because we have got to be back in an hour and a half, or my daddy might find out that I have taken more than a merely therapeutic or sympathetic interest in one of the patients under his care. He may find that out already," I add as an afterthought. Foo Foo is not likely to keep this under a veil of secrecy. "I can handle that, I think. But if you go batshit crazy out there by the fishing pond and try to gut me or something, I am going to have some explaining to do, even if I am able to restrain you and put you in the trunk and get you back on time."

She waves all that aside like so many flies. There is not going to be any scene like that. We get into the car and back out of the garage's shade. "You had better duck," I say. She kneels on the passenger's side floor mat, and we wheel on out. Near the gate, I see the old man from the waiting room. He is struggling to push a wheelchair laden with a big limp girl whose hands are pulled up against her chest like a squirrel's. I honk and wave to him as we cruise by. No recognition crosses his face. I see him shaking his fist in the rearview mirror as he shrinks.

"Whee," Virginia says, sitting up as we pull out onto the main road, and I stomp it. We are going eighty in no time, and the breath is getting sucked right out of us.

I forgot to bring worms or crickets. We find some night crawlers under a rock, and drop them into an empty coffee mug that was rolling around in the backseat. It is a piece of luck that the worms are so easy to find; I think it is because there has been so much rain. They stay closer to the surface in the daytime if there has been rain.

It turns out that Virginia has the fishing style of a purist. I had it once myself, but I have grown timid and more concerned with the number of fish I catch than the way I catch them. I swear I have drifted into middle age already, in a short twenty-two years. I am short on passion and drying up like drought corn; but that is the price of my pursuits.

There are two schools of cane-pole fishing. Both agree on the fundamentals of bait placement and bobber watching: You have got to know where the fish are liable to be, first of all, and the only way to know if you have got one nibbling is to watch the bobber. The line above the bobber is necessarily slack, so you cannot feel what is happening underwater, as you can on a spinning rod with a lure, or see the strike, as you can with a dry fly. Cane-pole fishing is all about local knowledge and paying attention, until you have got a bite, and that is where styles diverge.

When I see the bobber dip, I give the fish a second or two to get the bait and hook well into its mouth, and then I give the rod a little upward flick. It is a gentle movement. There is nothing in it but wrist. When the hook is set, I pull the rod around sideways and land the fish. There is not much to it.

Virginia's bobber drops, and she gives the fish the same second to get the hook in, but instead of the flick, she yanks the whole rod upward with her shoulders. That is how I used to do it when Papa would take me fishing when I was young and nothing was strange to me yet. Sometimes I would come up with nothing but bass lips to show for a whole afternoon, but when you do bring up a fish that way there is nothing like it. First there is a heavy resistance, like running a rigid hand, palm flat, through the water over the side of a trolling boat, and the rod bends close to breaking, and then the fish pops free and the pole goes straight, and the fish might end up on the bank behind you if you are smooth enough with your tug.

Virginia has got the true style. She pulls up a smallmouth. It must weigh two and a half pounds. That is no record, but it is a good fish on a cane pole. We have got six fish on a stringer I make with one of my shoelaces and two twigs before we put down the rods and fall to kissing on the mudbank, and then she pushes me off her and we lie back on our elbows, breathing hard.

"Whoo," I say, for lack of anything else.

Virginia laughs at me, and digs her fingers around in the worm can.

"So, Virginia," I say, "what brings you to Tuscaloosa?"

She smiles and dangles a worm from her fingers. "That's hard to say," she says. "It's fairly complicated. But I would say that the simple answers are love, hard living, and my father. In about that order."

"I see," I say.

"But I believe there may be a conspiracy afoot," she says confidentially.

"Is that so," I say.

"Yes," she says. "First of all, of course, I am not crazy."

"It doesn't seem so," I say.

"No," she agrees. "And also, some stuff has been taken that I think it will be hard for me to recover from the folks here."

"They keep it in a box," I say. "They give it back when you check out."

"We'll see," she says.

"Oh, they're good about it," I say.

"Anyway. I will be leaving in a few months," she says. "I will be eighteen, and what the asshole says will not matter." She pinches the head of the worm, or maybe the ass of the worm, and that end turns to paste. The other end keeps right on wiggling.

"How's that?" I ask. "I take it you are not at Branson by choice?"

"It's complicated," she says. "Until I turn eighteen, the fact that my dad says I am crazy is the law."

"Surely not," I say. "That's ridiculous." Until she turns eighteen. Oh, shit, I think. But then, I am no Methuselah, and I have committed no crime—yet, at any rate.

"I know," she says. "But if I leave before then, the cops will bring me right back. That's for sure." She smiles.

"They got you one time already," I guess.

"Yeah, boy," she says. The police in our town perform the duty of patient collection with some regularity. It is not too unusual for people to wander off, and we at the hospital have a cordial relationship with the police. Sheriff Hobson is one of the Doctor's good friends.

"So anyway," she says, "I guess I'm here until then."

"I'll ask my dad about it," I say.

"I don't like him," she says.

"Really?" I ask.

"It's not personal against you," she says.

"It doesn't matter," I say. "I'll have a word with him

anyway. Maybe you can work something out."

"Don't bother," she says. "I need the rest, anyway."

"Okay," I say, to that strange remark. She tosses the ruined worm out into the grass. Who knows? Maybe it will be able to grow back its squashed head, or its ass. I understand that worms are capable of miraculous acts of regeneration. It could start a new life underground, far from its old life.

I am still curious about Virginia's situation, though I do not want to pry too much. It sounds pretty odd to me, to be incarcerated because your parents decide you are nuts. But it is clear also, from Virginia's attitude, that she does not really want to effect an escape; she could leave right now, and she knows I would not move to stop her. Maybe she is just staying for the food and bed until she gets herself oriented, and maybe there is more to it than that. It could be that she is recovering from a breakdown; or perhaps, of course, it is all lies.

"If you don't mind my asking, Virginia," I say.

"What," she says.

"What did your father say was wrong with you?"

She sits up and bends her head around to look at me, fixing me with a pond-green eye. "He said I was a nymphomaniac," she says.

"Ah," I say.

"You know what that is, don't you?" she says.

"Yes," I say. "Is it true?"

"I'm not sure," she says. She lies back to take the sun, and closes her eyes. She appears to be at rest to me; the sun is hot, and she spreads her fingers from her hands, and her arms from her torso, and her knees drift apart. It is a position of calculated allure, under the cloak of enjoying the weather. She is an unusual girl, that is for certain. I find myself thinking of the fleshy mound of her vulva: how it must lie, curving upward, under the navy twill of the overalls, and maybe some panties. I reach to touch her bare foot.

When my hand comes to rest on it, Virginia's eyes open. That is the only movement she makes. I sit in the dirt, my palm pressed to the sole of her foot.

"What are you about there, Billy?" says Virginia, from way off where her head is.

"I am not so sure," I say. She holds really still, and I slide my palm up, over the lump of her ankle, and to the softly spiky fuzz of hair on her lower calf. Inappropriate thoughts flood in: I note that the hair is almost as long, but not as soft, as hair that has grown in completely. She has been at the hospital for at least a couple of weeks, but not much more.

I slide up the leg of my father's overalls. Red mouths, lips tightly pursed, run parallel to her Achilles tendon; I see that there are matching ones on her other ankle. You never know, until it happens, how something like that can darken your vision. I look around; I look up at Virginia and feel a hot shadow fall over both of us.

"Don't misunderstand, Billy," she says. "It was a long time ago. It had nothing to do with this. I feel much better now."

"That's good," I say. "I mean, I'm glad that you are feeling better."

"Please don't get all serious about it," she says.

"Okay," I say.

"Go on about what you were doing," she says.

"Maybe it is too quick," I say.

"It's not," she says.

I am afraid. I point up at the sky, as if to the cosmic clock, which ticks out our lateness. "We'd better head back," I say, and Virginia shrugs.

"All right, Billy," she says. "If you say so."

Virginia watches me clean the fish back in the cool of the garage. "Let me clean one," she says.

"Sure," I say. I have never really liked filleting fish. I always get stuck by a spine or cut myself, even with a sharp knife and good pliers. It is another one of those things I never quite get right. "Do you know how?" I ask.

"I've been watching you," she says. I lay down the knife, and she comes over to the board.

"Be careful," I say, as casually as you can say that.

The smallmouth that she caught, the biggest fish of the day, is the only one left to be cleaned. I watch over her shoulder as she makes the first cut, deliberately, forward and down under the lifted lateral fin, until the blade grinds against the bone. She keeps pressing down, and slices away the gill and a flap of the head, scraping off the eyeball with the tail end of her cut.

"Whoa, there," I say. The thin blood of the fish is smeared over her hand. She ignores me and flips the fish over. She stabs the point of the knife into the smooth side of the bass. It catches with a thump, deeply into the pine below.

"Fuck this fish," she says.

I reach for her smock, which is hanging on the hook where the overalls were, and she changes clothes again in the same way. I am filled with a vague shame, because I still desire her. I would like to have her right there, covered with fish guts.

"Hell, yes," I say. "That one was no good anyway." I walk her out the drive, and over to the hospital. "I'll be seeing you," I say at the door.

"Don't be a stranger, Billy," she says.

"Oh, don't you worry," I say. "There's no danger of that."

"For the most part, I had a real good time," she says, and goes up the stairs.

That evening, I consider the day's events.

"What you doing up there, Son?" yells the Doctor from the foot of the stairs.

"Reading," I yell, yanking the covers over my erection.

"Keep your hands on top of the sheets," he yells. "Can't have you going blind."

"No, sir," I yell, giving myself a little tap through the covers. It is no mean feat to keep a hard-on and converse with someone through a closed door and down a flight of stairs.

"I'm going out to a lodge meeting," he yells up. "Don't know when I'll be back."

"Okay," I yell. "Win big."

"Do what?" he yells.

"Nothing, have fun," I say. It is going to be a late night for the Doctor. His poker games at the sheriff's office often go until dawn. The picture of all those pale, fat men sitting around a metal desk smoking cigars and shooting the shit almost crowds out my pleasant thoughts, but I bear down and concentrate. I am back on track almost as soon as the sound of the Doctor's engine fades.

As soon as I am in a rhythm, however, a rock sails through the window next to my bed, showering me with shards of glass. I jump like a stuck shoat; as most people know, there is no time when a surprise is more surprising. When I collect myself and hobble over to the window, careful not to cut my feet, I can see Virginia's ghostly shape beckoning to me from the edge of the wood that abuts the backyard. My bowels go loose with the thrill of it.

I run down the stairs and out the back door, feeling naked as I cross the open space behind the house. My erection bounces in front of me, sliding against the fabric of my pajamas in a happily painful silky friction.

"Lordy," she says, when we are face-to-face in pines, the sound of our breath drowned by the screams of cicadas, "you come prepared."

"I was a Boy Scout," I say.

"You don't have to worry about me getting pregnant," she says.

"Me, either," I say, and we fall to, with a sweetness I have never known before.

In the small hours, when Virginia has gone back, I cut a piece of glass down in the basement and putty it into the hole in my window. The mess is cleaned up, and I am back in bed with the sky going gray through the new glass, before I hear the Doctor pull in.

Sunday I drive out to Peterson to see the Doctor's father. I bring Marmalade along to bolster the specious bond between us. She is more than pleased. She stands in the passenger seat and puts her front paws on the dashboard, smearing the inside of the windshield with dog snot and delight. "I wish you were in estrus, Marmalade," I coo. "I would make sure you got some from the old man's coon hounds."

The hills around Peterson have the geographic misfortune to be upriver from the papermill. At one time they were covered in a fairly dense growth of scrub pine. Agriculture was responsible for the clearing of a good percentage of the forest, and crops of cotton and tobacco, and peach and pecan orchards, cover the bottomlands, which are, by comparison to the hills, fairly fertile. The rest of the pine has been cleared in the last fifty years. Scrub pine grows extremely fast; if there had been even a modicum of thought put into the logging, the damage would have been minimal, but it did not happen that way. The forest was cut down in swaths a quarter-mile wide, and even bulldozed in places, so that the summer rains washed away the sandy red topsoil in great sanguine runnels before primary vegetation had a chance to take root. At this point, it is a practical impossibility for the forest to grow back as it was, or for anything at all to grow where it used to be. The Black Warrior runs a rich terra-cotta color when it floods. The land is bleeding away into the Gulf.

Papa lives at the top of a red knoll in a trailer. The Doctor has tried to get him to move closer to town, into one of the subdevelopments that he has got a finger in, but Papa will have none of it. He is a mean old drunk, in any case. I cannot see that any good would come of it, for him or the neighbors.

The gold Corvette he bought with the money from the timbering rights to his property is parked out in front of the trailer. The sun glances off its windshield in a white sheet. The fat tires are covered in dried red mud, as are the lower panels and exposed pipes. Papa is bent over by the dog run as I pull up. His worn pants are falling off his narrow ass. Marmalade scrambles out of the car when she sees the hounds in the run, and hurries over to say hello. They press their strange long faces to the chicken wire and go to baying. Papa slaps at where their noses protrude through the hexagonal holes, but they only back up to safety and keep it going.

"Hey, Papa," I call out.

"Hot enough for you?" he asks me. I nod. It is not one of those questions you actually answer.

"How you making out?" I ask.

"I'm tollable," he says, "but I be dog if the world ain't going to shit."

"You been watching that TV the Doctor gave you," I say.

"Hit were a radical Muslim on there when I turned it on this morning," he says, "jumpin around in a damn bathrobe."

"Muhammad Ali," I say.

"That's the one," he affirms.

"Well," I say. The years and the drink have been hard on Papa. His hide has been tanned, in the manner of roadkill, by the elements. As a young man he worked on the crews that built the highway from Birmingham. He knows how to drive a backhoe and slaughter a hog. These are skills that have not made it down to me through the generations. Sometimes at dusk, when a vague and wrenching sadness breaks over me, I am possessed of a certainty that if only I knew how to do those things, I would not feel as I do. No doubt this is incorrect, but I am unable to shake the romantic conviction that it is true.

"Well," he says. "Let's git on in out the sun." He points over at the run. "Them sumbitches dug themselfs clear out. I'm gitten too old to hunt." Two of them are already worrying the ground around the stakes he has driven through the chicken wire. They have the frantic singleness of purpose that only hounds can have. One lies in the far corner, ruminating on an exhausted work boot. "Ain't been out since you daddy come for em about a month ago."

"For what?" I ask. It is not hunting season.

"Hell, I don't know," says Papa. "He was with that sumbitch sheriff, Pete Hobson."

"Tracking down outlaws?" I ask.

Papa laughs. "I guess," he says. "That Hobson boy ought to be trackin' his damn self down. He's meaner'n a copperhead." There are few people of whom Papa does not have one opinion or another.

We walk on over to the trailer. The long room is cool and dark, with a brown shag carpet. The change in temperature and light give me the sensation of entering an underground cavern. There is a cold smell that is somehow both synthetic and earthy: maybe like a potted plant that has lain forgotten in the refrigerator for a few days.

"It's long past noon, ain't it, heh-heh," says Papa, pouring bourbon over two thermal plastic tumblers of ice. There is a wood grain embossed on the outside of the tumblers.

"Papa, it's almost dark," I concur.

"That's my boy," he says, handing me one. "Now what all you been about? You daddy says you done finished with the university."

"That's about the long and short of it," I say. "I'm mowing the lawn and running the lunatics on the grounds right now."

"Fit work for an educated man," he says.

"Yeah," I say. "Dad is trying to make me quit doing it. He figures I will not make my mark in the world with a lawnmower."

"Don't go gitten all wound up about it," says Papa. "It don't matter what you do if you got character."

"I guess not," I say. Papa scratches an armpit.

"You know what," he says.

"No sir," I say, "what's that?"

"I reckon it might seem to you like your daddy knows what he is doing, and that you should do what he says." This is not exactly how I feel, but I nod for him to go on. "You have got to ask yourself where you get your satisfaction, and do that thing."

"Yessir," I say.

"Now if you get your satisfaction from paperwork and lunatics, that is all right. But don't think that is the end of your options, boy," he says. "Take me for example. I get my satisfaction out of drinking. Just whatever you do, you got to go on and do it. If it is cutting grass, then that is what it is."

"I'm not sure that's what it is," I say.

"You're young yet," he says. "I weren't sure that drinking was my calling until I was a damn sight older than you."

"Yessir," I say.

"And it ain't about just having fun. That ain't it at all. It is about commitment, once you have got it figgered out what it is."

"The Doctor is a hard worker," I say.

"Shit," says Papa indignantly, "don't know hard work from nothing. He up and left when he was sixteen and made sumpin more of himself than I reckoned he would, but it all come easy. Ain't too much gone wrong for him since, except when you mama died. He was a goddamn All-American." This last is said triumphantly, as if driving home a point. It is a reference to my father's days on the gridiron. He actually played in the Rose Bowl when he was at the university, in one of those leather helmets that made the players look like muddy fighter pilots. It is another one of those things. However, I am not sure how it fits in.

"I guess so," I say. Papa's philosophy of work has either got some gaps in its logic or it is over my head.

"That Latham still workin at the hospital?" asks my grandfather. I know what he is getting at.

"Yeah," I say.

"That boy's a good un," says Papa. "Don't go disrespectin him. I known him since I was your age."

"He's about as dried up as you are, Papa," I say.

"Shit," he says. "He look a damn sight older than me."

"I don't know," I say.

"Well," he says. "I could use me a smoke." I shake a fat joint of Latham's pot out of my pack of Camels.

"I hear that," I say. "Miz Cutrell dropped in from next

door bright and early, and she had Jesus shining right out her butt."

"Good thing we got the antidope," he says. "I thought that sumbitch might have been creepin around the edge of my propity, but we going to smoke him out." He strikes a white-tipped match on the bottom of his cowboy boot and holds it out to me. I get it going and pass it over.

"Well, now," he creaks, before blowing a cloud of smoke out into the dark wet air. "You getting some, boy?"

"Oh, you know me, Papa," I say.

"You fixin to get married to that damn Brehard's girl?"

"I'm not fixing to do nothing," I say.

"That there's a double negative," he says.

"Well," I say. "College ain't what they crack it up to be."

"I know it," he says. "I got me a damn Corvette. But you listen here, son," he says, fixing me with a cracked, bloody, jaundiced set of eyeballs. "Ain't but one true path, and that's the one you on. Don't let nobody run you off it, and don't let nobody make you set down and stop."

"Okay," I say.

"You listening to an expert on free living," he says.

🍑

"Have you got the worms?" Daisy asks me.

"I have got the worms," I say. She is not the kind of person who goes fishing and forgets to bring the worms along.

The worms are cooling in their soup can at the bottom of the picnic basket. The picnic basket itself is a piece of work;

I have swiped it from the Doctor's ready supply of catalog-ordered outdoor equipment. It is a cube of light blue vinyl two layers thick, with a zipper running around three sides of the top face of the cube and a matching vinyl strap that runs from one top corner to the one diagonally opposite. The vinyl is patterned in a mock-canvas print. I think it is a handsome picnic basket, in its way, though the placement of the strap makes it a bit difficult to actually carry when it is full. One of the corners is always digging into you.

Daisy fetches the poles from where I leaned them against the wall next to the front door. The hooks at the free ends of the lines are tucked into the rings of bamboo at the bases of the poles, so that the lines are drawn tight and the poles bow slightly. Red and white bobbers, attached about halfway up the lines, shiver from side to side as she walks with the poles. She feeds the poles into the open rear window of her car, so that the tips stick out like two crazy antennae.

As we navigate the circuit of the round drive at the head of the entranceway, I see Virginia in one of the wicker chairs of the front porch of the hospital. Her eyes are on mine before I know what has happened. There is not so much as a smile or twitch of recognition as the long shining blue shape of the Buick slides through the frame of her vision. The way it feels to me is this: that I have just passed before an unmanned camera.

"Who was that?" asks Daisy.

"Just another goddamned lunatic," I say. Twelve bottles of beer are keeping the worms cool, and I reach down into the dark of the vinyl cube to find one.

There is the matter of busting Virginia out of the hatch on a regular basis. The night nurse in her wing, who had been dozing, caught her coming back in that first night we made love in the forest. Virginia played it off as another raid on the clotheslines, and the nurse, who I guess understands that kind of thing, decided to let it slide, provided that it does not happen again.

Virginia had the brilliant idea of complaining that her roommate's nightmares keep her from sleeping. She tells me that her doctor, Dr. Rosenthal, was all for putting her on some stronger medication to help her sleep, but she suggested that she be moved in with one of the vegetal cases just behind the fire door on the adjoining hall. Dr. Rosenthal was amenable. He is a Yankee. He is a supporter of the up-and-coming in mental-health care. He would like to see the patients taking a hand in their own recovery.

That is the way things are headed at Branson. Shock treatment is virtually a thing of the past, though the room is still set up for it, down in the basement. I used to sneak in through the cellar window and clap the wires to my temples. White hexagonal tiles covered the floor of the room and the walls up to a height of an adult's waist, and there was a brass drain in the center of the floor. I have no idea what the drain was for. I would make the noise "Zzzzzt!" with my teeth and tongue as I lay down on the leather-padded table. Cut loose from my moorings to the world of fact, my boat drifted on black waters, and I fished for leviathan sturgeons I could never raise. But as I said, those tools are practically artifacts. And the Doctor has not performed a lobotomy for three years.

Louise is the vegetal case into whose room Virginia is moved. I make a rope ladder that Virginia can keep under her mattress and throw out the window when I come for her in the night. Louise is not going to tell anyone about it. She has got cares of her own, I suppose. But her nightmares do not wake anyone up. Virginia is intrigued by her.

"Sometimes I open the window," says Virginia, "and let the wind wash over her. I think it makes her dream. And once I took my hand, and ran it across her breasts and the inside of her thighs, until she became warm and began to cough."

I tell Virginia she is wacky, but in a good way. She looks forward to the fall, when she expects to leave. She still declines to have me take up the matter of an earlier release with the Doctor; privately, I wonder if matters are as simple as she claims.

"Exactly what ails you, Virginia?" I ask. She is reluctant to say. I know that she is subject to the most severe depressions. The scars on her legs are testament enough to that, and I know that those times are not as far behind as she would have me think.

It is possible that my affair with Virginia is the most irresponsible activity in which I have ever engaged. Mental illness is funny until you have had a gander at it up close. There are entire halls of men and women here who do not relate to their worlds as humans. I can only imagine what it would be like to be trapped inside one of them. Some are bound hand

and foot at all times to prevent their doing themselves or others harm. They snap and snarl from cornered animal faces, or sit silent as stumps.

The Doctor brought me on his rounds when I was maybe five or six. I rode on his shoulders as we moved through the hallways, ducking under doorjambs. I was frightened when I looked into the eyes of the patients on the critical floors and recognized nothing familiar in them. The Doctor did not intend to frighten me, of course. He only wanted me to see what he did when he was at work in the big building, and perhaps to ease me into an understanding of the differences between people: how someone could be ill, but not lose their humanity to the sickness. But nothing like that happened. I wound my fingers tighter and tighter into the hair of his scalp, as if it were the mane of a horse that had gone off the path, out of my control, into a wilderness inhabited by the shadowy forms of monsters that were not quite recognizably human: half-people vaguely recollected from storybooks, satyrs and fauns and minotaurs.

The crickets in the jar swarm over one another in the filtered light of the moon. I have punched a pattern of holes in the lid to provide them with enough air to survive the night, and their bodies form a dimly seen orgy of spiked limbs and bulbous bony abdomens and heads. The horror of the cricket jar has never left me entirely; even after years of fishing with them I cannot bear to look when I reach in for one. I turn away and cup my hand against the glass, waiting for the unlucky one to find himself trapped under the fleshy dome of my palm and recap the jar as quickly as I am able. Virginia evinces no such fear of the crickets, and she slides them onto her hook with the assuredness of the expert: pressing the tip into the softly scaled swell of the abdomen's ventral side, forward just behind the rigid wall of the thorax, and out its front, directly aft of the frantically chopping lateral jaws, which find no purchase on the brass. A cricket so skewered suffers little internal damage. The metal of the hook lies between its external skeleton and what pass for its vital organs, and the cricket will twitch, submerged, until it suffers the dubious mercy of a fish, or finally drowns.

We have pirated an aluminum skiff, complete with a nine-horsepower Johnson, from the bank of the river just above the papermill. It is a shooting crime, but the fog lies so dense on the water that anyone giving chase would be bound to run into us before they saw us. We ran the boat against the current for half an hour, placing us, to my estimate, five miles and a long slow drift up from where we found it. The fog has an unusual effect upon the light that breaks through it, reflecting and refracting the moonbeams so that objects immediately close at hand, the edges of the boat, the white of the engine shell, the red of the old gas tank, are brightly lit, but beyond a few feet there is nothing to be seen. A world of whiteness gone dark presses all around, punctuated only by the sluggish ripples of the river and the muffled ringing thumps of our movements in the metal boat. The metal of the hull is chill and slippery, but I am not particular.

I would like to get intimate in this strange privacy; in fact, the crickets and spinning rods were no more than an excuse for this expedition. But it seems that Virginia is set on doing some more fishing.

"You'll get yours," she says. "I thought fishermen were patient."

"As a rule we are," I say, "but this is an emergency." She swats my hand away from where it has come to rest on her thigh.

"Hold up," she says. "I think I got something."

"You got a six-inch mamba coming to bite you is what you got," I say.

"You fuck off," she says. "I got me something bigger than that." Her pole is bent sharply and evenly down toward the water.

"It's a rock," I say. But we are moving with the current, albeit slowly, and the boat is not coming around as it would if Virginia were snagged. "Or an alligator," I whisper.

"Shut up," she says, and pulls back sharply on the rod. The drag is set lightly to make bringing in a catfish a little more fun, but whatever it is gives not an inch. The line slips out of the reel as she pulls, and she dips the rod and cranks the handle to bring it back in.

"Damn," I say, "maybe it's a big catfish. Set the drag a little tighter." She holds the reel over toward me, not moving her eyes from where the line disappears into the murk, and I adjust the drag. She reels in a little, and the line starts to come in. "Slow, or you'll break it," I say.

"Shut up. It's moving," she says, and indeed it is, whatever it is, moving around toward the stern.

"The prop," I say, and she holds out her arms straight, assuring clearance, and starts to reel again, and it is coming in slowly. She tells me to get the net, but there is no net. I was not figuring on landing anything this big. I hang my head over the edge to see if I can get a glimpse of it, but the water is like tar, and then the dome appears, and it is all clear.

"What is it?" she asks.

"A rock," I say, "with flippers."

"A turtle?" she says. "Shit, shit, a turtle."

It has got an ugly beak on it. A beak like that will make short work of a finger, or a half-inch oak dowel, for that matter. It looks at me broadside with its opaque reptile eye. She has got the rod bent steeply, and the turtle is suspended half in and half out of the water. It is a big one. In my mind it will grow to the size of a cafeteria tray. Prehistoric leather wings flap softly, tap-tapping on the boat, and its neck is craned out beyond normal extension: anything to ease the pain of the barb in its gullet. I grope around in the bottom of the boat until I find my knife, and grab the line carefully in my free hand, sliding down it until I am within half a foot of the gaping beak, and then I cut the line right where it exits the turtle. The turtle drops like an anvil out of sight.

"What have you done?" cries Virginia.

"I cut the line," I say.

"With the hook still in it?"

"I couldn't have got it out," I say. "It swallowed the hook."

"Swallowed the hook? Fuck you!" she cries.

"That's what I said," I say. "I'm sorry."

"Will it die?" she asks.

"I don't know," I say. "No, it will be fine."

"Liar," she says. "You should have killed it."

"I let it go," I say.

"You're a coward," she says.

"You would rather I had cut off its head," I say.

"That's what any sane person would do," she says. "Rather than let it swim around with a hook in its throat. Can you imagine that? A hook in your throat? Forever."

"Yes," I say.

"No, you can't," she says.

"I can," I say. "But it was a turtle."

"No," she says.

"It was a turtle."

"That's why you're good for me, Billy," she says.

"I am good for you because I lack the imagination to know what it is to be a turtle," I say.

"Yes," she says, and that is fine by me. I know that the turtle may well survive the hook. I also know that in this instance, Virginia has underestimated me. I have seen, under Papa's knife, the green curve of an ancient fishhook in the belly of a catfish, lodged there so long it had been subsumed into the flesh. The sight of it was more familiar than I can explain.

We have still got a long way to go until we reach the papermill, and she lays her rod aside and comes over to lean back against me. She pulls my arms around to cover her, and her shivering is gradually stilled by the warmth between our skins.

*chapter three*

How can he have been able to trail them? How, possibly, across a thousand miles of interstate? Papa said he took the dogs when he went. Not the same dogs, of course. It would have had to have been the sires and dams of the hounds, or maybe a generation earlier, even. Papa said he figured the Doctor took them for company, though what manner of man wants three howling, flea-infested blueticks for company is beyond me. Maybe he strapped one to the front bumper, head down, and followed its point all across the states of Alabama, Mississippi, Louisiana, and half of Texas. Whatever he did, he closed on them steadily, from the first mile. They were in sight at the end. I asked Papa, and he said the Doctor brought back the dogs and said, "I was this close." Papa held up his thumb and forefinger, real close together, for my examination. It was pretty close.

Papa says he chased her out of love, out of a broken heart. Fanny is not so sure. Why would he have brought the dogs, in that case? They are hunting dogs, after all. But Fanny is not likely to give me her real opinion on the matter. She just says, "I don't know, Billy. You know as much as I do now. Don't nobody know no more. I done told you everything. And don't you go telling him what I told you, or ask him no questions either. I didn't tell you nothing, remember that."

It was this way:

The Doctor came in one morning from a summer night out doing something with his father's coon dogs and found, instead of breakfast, a note on the refrigerator. The note does not survive, so I can only guess at its existence and contents; but there must have been one. I have thought of it often, of what it said, of how it was written. Did she scrawl it out in pencil on the way out the door? Did she compose it for months, revising and improving it over the course of long days in the carrel she kept at the university library, and type it up on one of the cranky old manuals they had lined up in the basement? Did she cry over it?

I doubt it. It was probably just a pithy little bolus of meaning, squatting there on the page, ready so long that when it was finally headed toward the paper, it was out of her before she knew it. There was a poem we had to memorize in high school, which almost everyone has heard. It is the William Carlos Williams poem about the plums, and it goes as follows:

*This Is Just to Say*

*I have eaten*
*the plums*
*that were in*
*the icebox*

*and which*
*you were probably*
*saving*
*for breakfast.*

*Forgive me*
*they were delicious*
*so sweet and so cold*

My English teacher told us that Dr. Williams left it for his
wife on the refrigerator one day, after he really did take
some plums out. Miss Cramer said it was dear to her
because it was a pure expression of meaning, without any
of the regular trappings of poetry; you can see that just
from looking at it. It looks almost like a couple of those
haikus strung together.

I imagine my mother's note was something like that, but
considerably less tender; despite its brevity and strength,
there is something tender about the plum poem. When my
father got the less tender refrigerator note, his first thought
was of the dogs he still had in the car.

The women must have put off a powerful smell, the way
they were all slicked up over one another. It was coming
off them like heat off a woodstove, the hot musk of their
lust. He did strap one of the hounds to the front of the car.
It was confused at first, barking dumbly and trying to lick
him as he tightened the cords around its fat, rabbitlike front
feet, and secured them to the bumper, and then made a slip
noose for the hindquarters. He tied the end of the slip
noose to the rear bumper, to keep the dog from sliding off

sideways. The hound was not uncomfortable. It takes more than that to make a hound uncomfortable; it was probably delighted, squatting up there like a lifesize drooling hood ornament. Until he put a pair of my mother's underwear up to its nose. Its eyes dropped out of focus, and it swung its head around, twitching its nostrils, as he drove in circles in front of the house, gripping the wheel impatiently, muttering "bitch, bitch," under his breath. The other hounds were all over the inside of the car, in his lap, bounding over the seat into the back, and then into the front. He struck out at them with his fist, stunning one. It sat still and panted happily, not hurt but slightly dazed, and then the one on the hood started up baying, and he hit the gas and was after them, stopping at intersections, following its point and frantic baying. The other two hounds were yelling, too, and there was nothing he could do to shut them up.

The Doctor was only eight hours behind. It was the start of day, and where the hail had lain, there were great puddles across the roadway that hissed and threw water up into the lead hound's face.

THE NEXT MORNING the fog has settled to knee height in hollows. Virginia is safely ensconced in the hospital, probably sitting bleary-eyed before a plate of bacon and pancakes, as I motor down the old highway toward Paradise. As I dip through a low spot in the road, where the fog still hangs, I hear, of all things, the pop of a turtle.

Box turtles (unlike the turtle of the river, which was broader and flatter and meaner, a snapper) undertake long, solitary pilgrimages in the summer. I have no idea what the reason is for these pilgrimages. I suspect that it has something to do with water or procreation or both, but that is no more than conjecture. For all I know there may be no reason at all for the pilgrimages; it could be that the turtles are lost. All I know is that for as long as I have been riding in cars, there has been the odd occasion when the vehicle will come to a section of roadway that has been selected for a crossing. One, or at most two, orange-and-black domes will be drifting across the asphalt with the stolid, unflustered aspect of Zen monks. These pilgrimages posed no danger to the survival of the turtles in preindustrial times, but in the New South they are suicidal. The box turtle, by virtue of its rigid carapace, can protect itself from the attention of any predator that it is likely to encounter, but its shell cannot save it from the danger of passing automobiles.

No one stops for a turtle. Lenny Hilgrew, who drove my hookup to high school, waged a veritable pogrom against the turtles; he did not stop short of backing up to go over one if he missed it on the first try. His fenders were often spattered with gore when he got done.

"Run!" I wanted to shriek, though I never did. "Run, run, before all is lost!"

They make a weird noise when you go over them. This is the popping sound I hear. The closest thing to it is the sound of a closed jar of mayonnaise hitting the pavement. There is the sound of impact, accompanied by a bona fide pop. A spasm of sadness clutches me when I hear the pop under my fat radial.

The ground fog clears from the road as I top a short rise and swing the wheel to the right, nosing the Cadillac onto a dirt trace. The great plane of the hood ducks and bobs in front of me like the deck of a ship, and the vegetation closes over in a canopy of greenery. It can get dark in the tunnel of a dirt trace, even on a bright day. The trees and vines have got a mind of their own. It is the mind of the tropical jungle: will divorced of reason. It closes over me with the thick sound of vegetal breathing—a choked and gasping hiss, neither in nor out, but a constant, circular osmotic movement of air and water through chlorophyllic fiber. And as the car bucks along up the stream of the red trace, deeper in and farther from the open blacktop and the cleared fields, there comes, behind the breathing of the plants and the rising and falling hum of the insects, a beat. At first it is indistinguishable from the organic sounds of the verdant underbrush, and then it grows and swells until it is too loud to ignore, and the trees part, and the car bounces out into a clearing of high grass, where old tires and oil drums lie dazedly about the base of a cinder-block hut that verily pulses in the heat and thump of the funk that blares tinnily out of a public-address system.

The hut was intended to be a church; services were held there when it was first built, and a cross hangs over the door-way still. It was painted the pink of strawberry sherbet years ago, but a tarry stain has crept down from the blackened brick of the smoking chimney, over the rusting roof, to form a dim plaque of barbecue goo on the pink cinder blocks. I can smell it as soon as the car is in the sun. There is nothing like it. I stop in the grass and put the car in park and head on over to the hut. There is a doorway, but I go to the square window. That is where you go to order.

Paradise serves only two kinds of food and one kind of drink. The drink is Coca-Cola, in ten-ounce green bottles. The corporate tentacles of that particular conglomerate have reached from Atlanta into jungles in Asia and darkest Africa. It is nothing to them to find their way to the remote wet corners of rural Alabama. Of course, Paradise has no liquor license. But paper cups are on hand, and even an ice-maker now, so you can mix your bourbon.

To eat there is meat and bread. The meat is pork, slow-cooked in the dark heat of the hole in the shack's back, and the bread is regular white bread, sold by the loaf.

Nigel's head appears in the square hole. "Bad Billy Mitch-ell," he says over the music, "how do you do?" We are sporting the same type of aviator glasses. An infinity of reflection, as appears in the opposing mirrors of a barbershop, springs up between us.

"All right," I say. "You keeping warm in there, Nigel?"

"They might be serving me up on white bread tomorrow," he says.

I order a pint of barbecue and a loaf of bread and a Coca-Cola. Today's meat is not ready to eat yet, but there are cardboard cartons of yesterday's leftovers sitting to one side of the ice in the dispenser, and Nigel takes one out and sets it to warm next to the pit. It does not make as bad a breakfast as you might imagine; you have got your protein and car-bohydrate, and Coke is better than coffee when the weather is warm.

Nigel also sells me a lid of the dope he and Latham grow. I roll some of it up, and we get high through the window. There is no one else working at Paradise, or any other cus-tomers this early in the morning; Nigel is there to get the fire stoked up and the new pork in the hole. My eyes become accustomed to looking into the darkness. I bob my head to the insistent rhythm, wiggle my fingers to the wailing guitar licks. The music calls out to some wilder place inside me. I do feel funky sometimes when I am good and stoned and there is a steady beat.

Talk turns to the war. I am almost old enough not to be drafted, and I was in college for the main years of my eligi-bility. The Doctor was going to make me join the National

Guard or something, but I never did get around to it. He served, and is not against my going if the situation should arise. I am not sure how I feel about it. On the one hand, it frightens me horribly. On the other, I could use some discipline. The death tolls in the paper make the war seem an unattractive way to come by discipline, but for some reason I feel a distance from the proceedings in the Orient. I have not known a dead person yet, personally.

Nigel has got a feeling. "My number be up soon," he says.

"Mine too," I say. It is possible.

"Shit," scoffs Nigel. "You ain't going to Vietnam, Whitey."

"I hope you're right," I say. "I got no quarrel with them Viet Congs."

The dark contour of his back is beaded with drops of sweat as he turns away toward the glowing, smoky hole in the wall behind him to turn a great blackened corpse over the embers. The muscles knot at his shoulders and around the lumps of his spine, throwing off the light and heat in slick, rounded highlights. I can imagine him creeping catlike in the night up a jungle footpath in Asia, an M-16 strapped to his naked back. He would be a formidable adversary. He would blend right in with the night and the foreign soil. Who knows of what acts of sure, confident violence Nigel is capable?

He comes back over to me and cracks a Coke open for himself. He takes a swig and gives me a playful punch on the shoulder, which jars me to my kidneys. I admit that I have some fear of him, now that he is three inches and thirty pounds bigger than I and has pink scar tissue all over the knuckles and backs of his dark hands, though he is always friendly, to a point. He is in business. It is unseemly to be overly menacing to a customer, and then there is the connection between our families. He may have his differences with his father, Caesar; in fact, I am fairly certain that they no longer speak to one another, but there is no getting out of your family. I do not care what they say about that. It is the truth.

I broached the subject of our common loss with him one time and received a less than favorable response. We were in junior high. It was one of the first times I got stoned, and he thought I was kind of an imbecile.

"We're almost like brothers, you know?" I said.

"You ain't never going to be a brother, Billy," he snickered. "I don't care how much you smoke."

"No, man, I'm serious," I said. "Because of our moms."

He looked at me as though I were a three-headed dwarf. "Just because our mamas ran off to lick each others' clits and got burnt up instead don't make us brothers," he said, which was a mouthful. I mean, we both knew it, even though our fathers had never mentioned it. Or at least mine had not. Fanny told me, under duress, when I was ten. She knew I would hear from somebody (Nigel, as it turned out), told me the truth, and made me swear not to talk to the Doctor about it. And I never have. It was not exactly public knowledge, but once I knew it, I could kind of tell that other people did, too.

Nigel and I sat there for a minute and let the conversational turd he had just evacuated lie there for a second, and then I went on. "No, man, I really see this," I continued. "It must

have shaped us, in the same way. We have parallel exis-
tences," I theorized, precociously cosmic. I was delighted
with my concept. "Kind of intertwined, and opposite, but
the same. Don't you feel that?" I said.

"No," he said.

"It was just an idea," I said. We sat around for a while.
"Do you think about them?" I asked.

"Will you shut up, Billy?" he laughed. "All this remember-
this, imagine-that shit is stupid."

"I think about them," I said. "I can't help it."

"What do you think?" he asked.

"They're driving west," I said.

"Are they nekkid?"

"No!" I said. "At least not usually," which sent him howling backward off the fender we were sitting on. I think this
would have been a heavier conversation if either one of us
could remember our mothers, or if we were talking to someone else about it. We were like amputees, laughing at
wooden-leg jokes. "It's this heavy thing," I said, "this huge,
paranoid, triumphant vision," which sent him, where he was
lying in the dirt, into another fit, and I gave up on trying to
explain it. It is not the kind of thing you can talk about and
make much sense, anyhow.

I guess it is not too strange that Nigel and I have never
really met over the circumstances of our childhoods. People
deal with things in different ways. Nigel remains something
of a mystery to me, despite my familiarity with the facts of
his personal history.

Nigel is the youngest of four children, the first three by
another woman from whom Caesar was estranged before he

married Carmen. He never took a third wife. The others are considerably older than Nigel and I, practically adults during our childhood, and share with one another the porpoiselike brow of their father. I heard at one point a strange piece of information, the veracity of which I have no reason to doubt: that if Nigel's attendance records were eliminated from the rolls, the Rathberry family's attendance record and performance at school would be the best of any family's in central Alabama. All three missed something like four or five days in total, and were awarded all manner of prizes and scholarships.

Caesar has been saved by Christ. I believe he came by his association with Jesus late in life, after the death of his wife; certainly he did not meet Him through Latham. I have to wonder how much comfort He has brought Caesar, who frankly makes me nervous. Caesar has an uneasy, close-throated exhortatory tone when discussion meanders toward things divine, and a deliberate way with the use of a re-proachful, knowing, nearly violent silence in the presence of conversation and attitudes clearly entrenched in a secular worldview.

I have felt the chill outskirts of this dread quiet at its most intense only two times. The first time was when I was barely ten years old and out back behind my grandfather's old house (since burned down) with Nigel. I had just received a BB-gun for my birthday, and we were taking turns shooting at a goat that was penned up in what had been a pig run. It was a tough old goat; once I had seen one of my grandfather's coon hounds make the mistake of clambering over the fence to harry it, and it butted the dog up against the wires and cut up the dog's head pretty bad with its spiky horns and hooves before I ran for my grandfather and he dragged the dog out.

So Nigel and I were hidden from the goat's sight behind a woodpile, and the old yellowed billy could not figure out the cause of the shocks of pain that were lighting up along its hide. As each pellet went home, it laid back its ears and flinched and skipped, the vector of the pain gradually herding it toward the corner farthest from us. Its eyes were rolling weird enough to show some white. It was a little bit broadside, and it seemed to me as though the near eye were looking right into mine over the notch in the sight. The pellet hooked, and I got it one time on the nose so perfectly that I think it figured everything out, and turned away from us and faced into the far corner. It crunched itself up as small as it could get, ratty goat tail quivering and curving down toward its pendulous scrotum, and its head tucked away where we could not get to it. We were laughing fit to bust, and I took another shot at it, and it just dropped as dead as a stone.

When it keeled over, we both stopped laughing. I had that feeling of suddenly needing to defecate. It seemed that all the noises on the farm erupted into silence. I remember putting down the gun quickly: throwing it, even, as if to proclaim my innocence with the distance I put between myself and the toy rifle. The strangest part was that when we climbed over the fence and examined the carcass (and it was a carcass; I have seen no deader goat before or since), we could not find a single hole in the goat's hide. There was not a solitary mark on it that might have been made by the brass pellets. And of course that makes perfect sense; you can kill a small bird with a BB-gun, but even a good one with ten pumps in it will barely penetrate human skin at twenty feet, and we were farther than that from the goat. There is no way my shot went through the goat's flank and penetrated to a vital organ; it would have had to have tunneled through fifteen or twenty inches of bone, muscle, and goat gristle to get to the heart or lungs.

I was on my hands and knees running my fingers along the cooling haunches of the billy goat when Nigel snickered and touched my cheek. "In its butt," he said. "You shot it in its butt." And I had the tail in my fist and was peering into the furry whorl of the goat's anus to see if there was any sign of my pellet having entered there when we both became aware of Caesar's erect figure standing by the side of the house. I don't know how long he had been watching, but I believe that he saw the whole thing. We slunk over to where he stood, and he was positively trembling with anger.

"Savages," was all he said, with a long hiss at the start, and the consonants all running into one another so close it sounded like a word from some utterly alien language. It looked to me as though the whole inside of his eyes had gone red between the iris and the black of his skin as he glared down in judgment at us over the angry flare of his broad nose. He did not say another word to me, but turned on his heel like a military man and walked back around to the front of the house with Nigel following him without a backward glance. The stiffness of Caesar's back as he goose-stepped away positively violated the natural curvature of the spine. I heard his rattletrap car cough and spit to life and hack its way out to the road, where it drove away slowly, soberly, in measured fury.

I was convinced for some time that Nigel's theory of death

by BB in the butt was correct, and when I tell the story that is still the way I end it. But of course that is so improbable as to be an impossibility. Even if the pellet had entered there, it would not have made it past the goat's intestines. I believe that the goat died of a heart attack at the exact moment we chose to be shooting at it, or that it died of shame. Whatever it was, I caught hell for it.

Nigel lifts his elbows from their resting place on the counter behind the window and withdraws into the hut. He gives the meat a casual poke and comes out the side door to join me in the sun. It is turning into a regular summer day; the sky is colorless and low, without clouds. Bobwhites would whistle from the electric lines that cross over the meadow if we could hear them over Parliament's galactic grind; they perch, fat and still as cantaloupes except for the amphetamine twitches of their tiny heads.

A swarm of purple martins explodes from the woods over by the road back out of the glade, ushering in the blunt nose of a patrol car. It bucks implacably toward where we stand, stoned, against the pink wall. I think to myself that an ounce of pot makes a mighty big bulge in a pair of khakis. As the black-and-white pulls even to us, we can see the two cops inside; the driver's muscular arm hangs out his window. Sunlight bounces from the crystal of his watch and the chrome of the searchlight bolted to the windshield support. They pass in slow motion, close enough that we can see the reddish down on the near cop's wrist, and the knurl on the pump of the shotgun propped against the center of the dash.

I nod and smile, but they roll on impassively, and make a circuit of the building. When they pass out of sight behind the hut, Nigel spits meditatively and shakes his head to my questioning look. The patrol car drives back across the meadow and into the greenery, and the martins flurry again, and settle.

"That was a close one," I say, relieved. Nigel shrugs. "Do you think they're onto you?" I ask.

"Onto me?" he says.

"The dope?"

"Maybe," he says.

"The pigs," I say, shaking my head.

"Yeah, the fucking pigs," he says. "I'll bet you hate those fucking pigs."

"Sure," I say. "I say legalize it."

"It ain't about that, Billy," he says. "How do you go to college and get so ignorant?"

"What's it about then?" I ask.

"It's political, man," says Nigel, dismissively. "You'd better get on out of here."

"What," I joke, "are you running for mayor?" He leans back against the bricks, which are the last cool thing, and laughs.

"Yeah, that's it," he says. "You looking at the next mayor of T-town."

"You've got my vote," I say.

"That's great, Billy," he says. "Now you had better head on home."

He goes back into the hut as I get into my car. The leather

of the seat scalds my back between my belt and where my shirt rides up. I holler, "See you later," as I put the Eldo into gear, but I guess he does not hear me.

🍑

It is as much a surprise to me as to anyone that I become jealous of Virginia's sexual past. She will not tell me anything about it.

"What was it like your first time?" I ask.

"I broke him in half," she says. "I wrecked him."

"You did."

"Yeah, boy," she says, "like an old stick."

"Who was it?" I ask.

"You don't know him."

"Of course I don't—you're from Memphis."

"But who?"

"Yeah."

"My daddy."

"Oh."

"I'm just kidding you, boy," she says. "For real? . . . It was my pet boa constrictor."

"I suspected as much," I say. She does not ask me a thing.

🍑

Finally it works out so that Virginia is on my work crew one day a week. It does not take too much lobbying on her part to get Dr. Rosenthal to see the light on that point. I imagine he is just tickled pink to have her all raring to go to get outside and do something productive. I figure he has got no idea about our midnight liaisons. He has a little chat with me, in the shadow of the arch you drive through to get to the central courtyard. The fan of finger-chopping fame whirrs behind his head, sucking the breathed air out of the hospital and blowing it across us through the protective grating. Dr. Rosenthal has his back to the fan. His hair, thinning and fine and pale, blows forward at me like the foam off a wave. He raises his voice to be heard.

"Billy," he says, pulling me into his shoulder with the handshake and speaking toward my ear: a gesture of fraternal confidence, "this girl Virginia." It makes me nervous.

"Yeah?" I ask.

"I'm not sure how stable she is. You know what I'm saying?"

"Sure," I say.

"Of course you do," he says. "You've been around the patients your whole life. But just remember, we're only a yell away. If something should happen."

"Like what?" I ask.

"Nothing you can't handle. A fit. Acting strangely. Non-cooperation. Anything like that."

"Actually I've met her before. She came by and stole a dress from my next-door neighbor's line," I say. We chuckle.

"I remember," says Dr. Rosenthal.

"She's cool," I say. "We'll be fine."

"Okay," he says.

"But I'll let you know," I reply. "If there's anything out of the ordinary." He nods at me with seriousness that was once calculated and has become habitual. I think I could have liked Dr. Rosenthal a few years ago, when he came to Branson freshly educated and eager to work hard and do good. He has got the same intentions still, but he has taken the blows of repeated failure, or at least lack of progress, that are the background to state mental care. Dr. Rosenthal has made the shift from idealism to dismay, but he has not come around to taking things philosophically.

As it turns out, Virginia and I have a big time working together. There is something about the smell of it, the dirt on her hands and knees and mine, driving into the creases of our skin, stinking richly a little bit of cowshit Latham and I spread around the rose beds right at the start of spring when we were sure there would not be another frost, the smell of the soil mixing in with sweat and how a scalp smells when it has been under the sun: I secretly nurse an erection under the fabric of my dungarees as we crawl around between the bushes, plucking out weeds.

There is no need for us to make a great show of not knowing one another, though of course we cannot touch more than incidentally.

Bees circle as if blind, nuzzling the hot blossoms in search of points of entry. Earl, the boy who was stung a week ago, seems uncomfortable to me, and I crawl his way to see how he is doing. The bees orbit his head too closely. It may be that he smells good to them, that they are looking for points of entry. The idea of insects crawling noisily into nostrils and ear canals gives me the willies. It may be something else: It may be that they can smell his fear and close in on it like sharks on a bleeding fish. The Doctor taught me young that there is no harm in dogs or horses, unless they know you are afraid. "Pheromones, boy," he said to me. And, like him, I have never been bitten or thrown.

"Just relax, Earl," I say, adopting a soothing voice. Doubtful and fish-eyed, he cranes his neck at me. I can tell that he is forcing himself to be careful with his movements: that he is making every effort not to disturb the space around him, trying even to physically shrink. A slick of sweat darkens the lank hair behind his ear. "Do you want to go in?" I ask. He shakes his head no, shamefully. There is nothing I can do for him.

Virginia, when I crawl back to her, has got a darker look than when I left. I have seen this before, when she jammed the point of the knife through the bass. An opacity clouds her eye: curtains dropping heavily and without noise behind glass. I have been only five feet away and for no more than half a minute.

"Hey," I say. She moves her mouth into a smile, but it is malformed by the set of her jaw, which lies slack behind closed lips, as if she had a mouthful of something she was trying to hide. I move in closer. "Hey," I say again, and it looks to me as though the set of her forehead relaxes, and she leans in, almost as though for a kiss, and opens her mouth. I see in shadow behind her teeth, on the wet pink of her tongue, a furred shape slowly crawling back toward her throat, and as I pull my head back in instinctive recoil she moves in closer, her face swelling horribly toward mine, and it turns and buzzes and flies at my face, bouncing madly against my forehead as my heart bursts up toward the top of my head, and my body rings with adrenal shock.

We sure do have a big time.

But there is no way Dr. Rosenthal is going to hear about it. I cannot have her put under closer supervision.

It is an unfortunate juncture we have reached. I am falling for a lunatic. She says she is not sick, that she is getting well, but I know better. There is Dr. Rosenthal's concern, and there is what I see for myself, the eyes just shutting down. There is nothing that will break you like loving a crazy person. I do not know it from experience, but I have seen them, the loved ones, the mothers and fathers and wives and husbands.

Farm dogs bark in the dark as we fly by. Virginia and I are on the road, driving homeward from another night on the riverbank. Dawn is not showing to the east yet, but the tweet-tweet of the first birds from the roadside has joined the chorus of frogs and bugs. Lack of sleep is wrecking me. It is not that I would change things, not at all. It is just that between my duties on the grounds and my pleasures in the night, there is little time for rest.

A lone black man screams by us at the top of his highest gear on a lightless motorcycle, just before we drift back into the city limits. Virginia turns and watches him recede into the distance.

"I'm going to get me one of them things," she says, "some-day."

"Good clean fun," I say.

"I love it," she says. "Ain't a thing that can catch you."

"You know how to drive them?" I ask.

"You bet, son," she says. "I stole my daddy's one time and come back a week later."

"Wild," I say. "You are a wild one."

"I reckon so," she says. "At least, so it has been said before." She snatches at the wheel, yelling, "Watch out Billy!" I had been looking at her while she spoke, and almost drifted off the shoulder and run over Nigel Rathberry himself, who is jogging toward where I have stopped. He is a tad bit wild in the eye. Nobody wants to get hit by an Eldorado.

"I'm sorry, Nigel," I apologize. "I didn't even see you."

"Can't you see darkness in the night?" he says weirdly.

"What," I say, and Virginia giggles.

"Can we give you a lift?" she asks politely.

"Yeah," he says, "you can give me a lift." He asks me if I mind if he drives, and I say no, and he comes around to my side. I look up at him and over at Virginia, and she is making no move. I slide from behind the wheel and into the back. It is strange to be in your own car when someone else is at the wheel. The dashboard, the hood, all the shapes and spaces, seem different when you are sitting in a different seat. I never noticed that there are ashtrays in the back seat, nestled into the armrests, just like in the front. This is the asinine thought I am thinking when Nigel pulls a squealing U-turn and fishtails the car back in the direction we came from.

"Whoa," I say.

"Did you see a motorcycle?" he asks me over his shoulder.

"Yeah," I say, "going this way."

"Nigger left me," he says. We are hauling ass back up the highway.

"We can catch him," I say.

"I'll catch him later," says Nigel. "No need to worry about whether I catch him." He is looking at me in the rearview mirror. "Get out the way, boy," he says.

There are lights behind us in the distance. Nigel glances nervously at them, and then at the speedometer, and after a moment of deliberation pulls back on the gas pedal until we are going something in the vicinity of the posted limit.

"We can outrun them," I say.

"Shut up. Shit," he moans, "why am I driving?" But it is too late for a stealthy switch. He tells me to quit looking back. I lie down on the seat, wondering what kind of mess I have just gotten myself into. I need to get Virginia back to the hospital. She is not listening to him, telling her not to look back, and smirks down at me. Her face gets brighter and then white as the other car pulls right up on our tail, and then she actually waves at them as they pass.

"What the fuck is wrong with you?" Nigel says to her as I pop back up and do not say a thing about the red lights shrinking ahead of us.

"I was just waving at the man in the window," she says.

"Shit," says Nigel, and that is about it until we take a couple of turns I do not know, and Nigel gets out and says he owes me one, which I figure is about right. I take the wheel and hurry us back, afraid of the light in the east.

"I know what you wish," says Virginia.

"What do I wish?" I ask. I am beat. All this excitement is taking it right out of me.

"You wish you were him," she says.

"Nigel?"

"You wish you were him, all strong and black and running from the law like a sexy bandito."

"I do not. He is a mere hooligan. Did you say that was the law?"

"You just wish you were," she says. "But I like you all right anyway."

"Who was in the car, Virginia? Was that the police?"

"It was your daddy in the car," says Virginia.

"I doubt it," I say. "It's four in the morning."

"Him and three others," she says.

"Three other whats?" I say.

"Three other white men," she says.

"White men in the night," I say, "giving chase to a mysterious sexy bandito."

"You call it what you want," she says.

"You call it what you want," I say. "I believe you have made a mistake."

"I have made them before," she says, "but this ain't one of them times."

His car is not in the driveway when I pull in and creep up the stairs for a couple of hours of sleep. But then, he could be out giving comfort to some widow or divorcée. I do not meddle in his affairs.

The Doctor's summons arrives in midafternoon, when I am in the toolshed marveling over my latest acquisition as head groundsman: some sort of weed-whacking mechanism. It looks like an electric trolling motor, the kind you bolt to the front of your fishing boat and lower when you want to navigate marshy patches or move quietly at low speed, but instead of a propeller this thing has got an eight-inch length of twenty-pound test. I pull it to life and almost whip my feet off at the ankle. It is the kind of thing you have to be careful with.

Latham looks at it doubtfully. "He said for you to go see him in his office," he says.

"What about?" I ask. Latham shrugs: a stupid question. He takes the whacker from my hands and test-drives it on the tall grass snuggling up against the side of the shed, a cigarette hanging off his lip, and then makes a circuit of the shed. When he appears at the other side, I can see from his expression that it is a sorry day for the weeds at Branson. He gestures at the hospital with the whirling end.

"Get on," he says, and I tuck in my shirt and head over. I can see the Doctor's wing tips on his desk before I can see the rest of him, but he knows I am there. Maybe he smells me.

"Come on in," he says. I step in, and he tells me to shut the door, which I do with my best casual deference.

"Hi, Dad," I say.

"Hi, Billy," he says. "You want to set down?" I say sure and pull a chair up to the front of his desk, where I am facing right into the soles of his shoes. They are in good shape, with a high polish on the uppers that picks up the sunlight coming in from behind him. He squints at me. "How many times I got to tell you about them sunglasses, boy?" he says, and I take them off and hang one arm down the front of my shirt collar, in a hurry.

"I just forget I'm wearing them."

"Are you fixing to get yourself into a heap of shit?" he asks.

"I hope not," I say.

"That's good," he says, "because last night I thought I saw something strange. I thought I saw a nigger who will remain nameless at this time driving your car with a pickled blonde riding shotgun."

"In the Eldo?" I say.

"I guess not," he says.

"I was home," I say, "asleep."

"I just couldn't figure it out," he said.

"What were you doing?" I ask.

"Ain't none of your business," he says, pointedly. "But since I am setting here prying into your business, which is not my business, I will tell you that I was busy taking some money off the sheriff and some other no-accounts in a poker game."

"Oh," I say.

"When I heard one of them dirt bike two-strokes kick up and tear out of there, and we look out the window and the damn patrol car was burning like to blow up." My father is grinning. "You should of seen that damn Hobson," he says. "First he drop a hundred dollars on your old man, and then he look out the window and his damn car's on fire. Apo-goddamn-plectic. He just grabbed his gun, and we went trying to chase down the bike, and that's when I passed the car."

"You catch him?" I ask.

"Nah," he says. "But I got my hundred dollars."

"Well," I say. We sit there for a while.

"I guess you got to be going," he says. "I can hear that grass growing." Marmalade is tugging at my pants legs with her tiny teeth, and I bend down to pat her. She is a pathetic little wretch.

"I guess so," I say.

"I didn't mean to be getting in your affairs," he says. "I just couldn't figure it out." I shrug. "Politics is a bad business, boy," he says, obscurely.

"I know it," I say.

"How about that, though," he says, "a Cadillac and a blonde."

"It's legal," I say. "Who was it?"

"Who?"

"In the Cadillac."

"It don't matter," he says. "You don't know him."

As I consider my interview with my father, Fanny makes peanut-butter sandwiches. Her hand with the knife goes scoop, spread, slap, as she looks out the kitchen window. She places a pile of them on the table, on a yellow plate.

"Milk or tea?" she asks.

"Tea," I say.

We eat the sandwiches, thick ones on Wonder, and wash them down with sweetened, clove-flavored tea mixed with lemonade. I follow Latham's distant progress with the weed-whacker by its rising and falling whine, which comes in through the open window along with a squadron of flies that circle, loud as helicopters, occasionally settling on the shrinking pile of sandwiches.

The Doctor does not trust me; otherwise, why would he lie to me about Nigel? There is no doubt in my mind that my father recognized him in the convertible. He as much as said so during our chat.

The more pressing questions are whether my father recognized Virginia, whether he thinks Nigel had anything to do with the burning car, and whether he thinks I have anything to do with either one of them. It is a veritable ball of cottonmouths, as problems go; you cannot see the head of one part of it for the tail of another. Maybe there is nothing to worry about at all, for me; it sounds like the Doctor did not identify Virginia, and that is my primary concern. In addition, they would have pulled Nigel over, and maybe killed him, if they thought he was the perpetrator. Hobson is not a man to take arson lightly.

So I guess I can go about my business, though this entire episode has given me the willies. I do not want any part of this kind of nonsense. I want only my leisure to reflect, and Virginia.

Still, I return to the fact of my father's lie. Perhaps his motives are pure, and he wants only to protect me from involvement in whatever strange feud is being played out between the more dangerous characters of the neighborhood. Then again, perhaps he is more involved in it than I know, and is uncertain of my allegiance. For all of our living under the same roof all these years, except for my tenure at the university, we do not know one another so well. He must realize that I have doubts about his nature, but can he guess what intimations I have had in dreams? How can I know whether I am finding my way toward a conjunction of real history and the moment, or losing myself in an imaginary landscape, where the landmarks dissemble and signposts spin with passing breezes, pointing to different destinations each time the traveler returns to the crossroads?

The burps of the papermill, as usual, linger over downtown. It is not a problem to find a parking space in metropolitan Tuscaloosa, especially in the summer. The students from the university have all gone home, and the stores along Broad Street shut their doors to the brown heat of the outside and settle into the dead indoor cool of summer. Town and Country Clothiers is not a place I spend much time, but Mrs. Klopine recognizes me the second I walk in. It must be my striking good looks. She bobs a pyramid of lavender-tinted hair at me. I nod back at her, with an affected shoe-scuffing adolescent clumsiness. It is my opinion that these older women like it if you act as though you are not quite as clever as you really are and trip on the occasional doorjamb.

"What can we do for you, Billy Mitchell?" she says. Eunice, the junior salesperson, gets her powdered butt off the stool behind the glass counter and comes over to join Mrs. Klopine in her examination of me.

"Why, you've gotten as good-looking as your daddy," Eunice says. I find this slightly disagreeable. The Doctor is a handsome man, I acknowledge, and I have inherited his aristocratic jawline, but Eunice is no older than I am. The sparkle in her eye gives me a queasy feeling. It could be that the Doctor did. I would not put it past him.

"Hi, Eunice, Mrs. Klopine," I say. "I come to get me a dress."

"I think we just might have a baby doll that would show off those pretty thighs of yours," Eunice says, pinching my cheek and giving it a good shake.

"Why, Eunice," says Mrs. Klopine, "you cut that out. Our Billy is not wearing dresses."

"No, ma'am," I concur.

"It's a gift, isn't it, honey?" she says. That Mrs. Klopine is a sharp one.

"Yes, ma'am," I say. "For my sweetheart."

"You are so sweet," she says.

"Yes, ma'am," I say.

"Why, that's the tackiest thing I ever heard of," bursts out Eunice. "You should know better, Billy Mitchell."

"What is?" I ask, as Mrs. Klopine purses her lips at her assistant.

"Buying your girl a dress!" she says. "Who all raised you?"

"Eunice!" says Mrs. Klopine.

"There's some real nice scarves and jewelry here," says Eunice, "from New York."

"I'm looking to buy a dress," I say.

"For Daisy Brehard?" says Mrs. Klopine.

"Why, you know everything, don't you, Mrs. Klopine?" I say. She wipes that aside with a flutter of a manicured, blue-veined hand and a skyward roll of her eyes.

"It so happens that we have her size on file," says Mrs. Klopine. "But don't you think maybe a nice hat?"

"Now that's a sweet thought," I say, "but I want to get a dress. That shows her shoulders. I'm just wild about her shoulders." Eunice shakes her head. She is not used to dealing with trash like me.

"That girl has the most lovely shoulders," says Mrs. Klopine. "Skin like hers is a sign of good breeding."

"That's what I always say," I agree. I finger the hem of a black dress on the rack nearest me. "Is this one in style?" I ask.

"If you're going to a funeral," says Eunice.

"We're not," I say.

Mrs. Klopine takes me over to a rack of sunny dresses that are not made out of too much cloth. "Now what kind of function are you all attending?" asks Mrs. Klopine.

"One of them Dionysian Rites," I say.

"Ooh-la-la," she says. "Is that what the committee is calling them this year?"

"Yes, ma'am," I say. "They are making their debut in the style of the ancient Greeks."

"You are a card, Billy Mitchell," she says.

"The Joker, haw-haw," I say.

We work together and pick out a white number that is going to look just right on my Virginia. I can see it already, peeling off of her in the backseat. I have a hard time of it getting those women to believe that Daisy is a size six, though. "That girl is a ten if I ever did see one," declares Eunice.

"She ain't had nothing but pot likker for a week and a

half," I say. "It's coming off of her like icing off a cake in the rain."

"Well, you tell her she can return it if it doesn't suit," says Mrs. Klopine.

"Yes, ma'am," I say. I pay in cash.

Everything is just as right as it could be, though, when I go knocking come midnight. I will admit to a fondness for these ground-to-window rendezvous. She tosses up the pane at the sound of the first pebble cracking against it. "Rapunzel," I hiss, and the rope ladder comes tumbling down as sweetly and softly as a loosened skein of tresses. Virginia is on the ground in no time. She has got an athletic streak.

"What you got in the bag?" she asks me.

"A dead groundhog," I say. "If you be good, I'll let you eat some."

"You are too thoughtful," she says. When she sees the dress, she is pleased, though. I have been doing some thinking about that. The dress, I mean. It is my hope that the dress will have significance for Virginia beyond its value as an object. There is more than my prurient interest in seeing her decked out sexy at stake, too. No matter what people say, there is something about being forced to wear a certain costume that makes you feel like you are what you have been dressed up as. I have seen this at work my whole life. Some of the afflicted at Branson were making it, or almost making it, out in the world of solid people. When they put on scrubs for the first time—scrubs, that is what those aquamarine hospital pajamas are called—they became ghosts, or animals, or something just a little bit less than human.

I am not saying the outfits are not necessary. Scrubs set up a duality between the sick and the well that is indispensable at an institution the size of Branson. There is no way to manage the legions of fools as individuals—not really. They have got to be lumped together into some kind of easily directed, homogeneous flock. For them to be helped (and for a good number of them the help they need is strictly material and managerial, someone putting three hot meals down their throats and shuttling them from bed to rec room to shower to bed), the depersonalization that occurs when they are institutionalized is an unavoidable evil.

But I hate to see it happening with my Virginia. My Virginia. The name, ever since it first fell on my ears, long before I met the Virginia in question, has always been the cause of two simultaneous and contradictory reactions in me. It excites me. The sound, "Virginia," with its softly furred consonants and phonetic resemblance, has always reminded me of vaginas—even before I actually encountered a vagina, I believe my conception of them was colored by the sound of the word. And then there are the more traditional meanings suggested by the name, which make me sad and reverent: purity; untraveled, untrammeled land; and a holiness, even. Now I cannot utter the name without a loss of breath, without some strange, unspoken pang clawing at my entrails. I do not know if this pang is a normal reaction: if it means simply that I have fallen in love. Some of what I have read would lead me to believe that. I think, however, that an urgency hovers about my feelings for Virginia that is outside the bounds of common rapture. That is because, of course, of the tragic dimension that our love affair will have to take. Even now there is something of a tragic air about it; the inevitability of disaster accompanies us on every tryst, like a third party forever begging to gain entrance into a secret shared by two.

At any rate, I am in a hurry to see her in the dress. It gives me no pleasure to see her wearing the duds of a lunatic. I think she would be less likely to slip away (from the firm ground of optimistic sanity, not her hospital room with the comatose Louise) if she were given the opportunity to pretend a certain amount of normalcy in the moments it might or might not exist: because those are most of the moments, for her. She is not what you would call plumb nuts, but she is not what you would call completely levelheaded, either. She is on the fence. It just depends upon which way she is looking.

She wants to go away in the car, so we hustle on over to the garage, taking the approach tree by tree. The Doctor is out at one of his poker games at the sheriff's. I hope he is wearing a flak jacket; the station is getting to be a hazardous place.

We make love on the bank where the Black Warrior laps turbid and warm against a gravel bar, with the dress up around her armpits. We are shielded from the road by a screen of pines, but we are wide open to the river. And sound carries like crazy across water. It is uncanny, the distance you can hear across water at night. The idea of some kids fishing on the far dark bank and hearing the dim, partly stifled cries of our passion is aphrodisiac to me: too much so, it seems. Her hair is barely messed up before I spend myself inside her.

"That's okay, Billy," she says.

"I love you," I say.

"I know," she says. "That's why you're going to take me away."

"Oh, Virginia, you know I would," I say, "if you weren't crazy."

"You the one crazy," she says. "Crazy about me."

I have not got much to say to that one. It pretty much puts us where we are at. She is crazy, and I am whipped. I would like to take her away and set ourselves up somewhere where the Doctor could never find us, and the specters of her past and craziness could never follow—somewhere where the air is clean and there are hills bigger than the Moundville Indian Burial Graves and the wind blows in bright off the ocean, never yet touched by human tongue or lips or lung. That is what I would have for us, if I could live in the world of my design. But we are five miles north of Tuscaloosa, with one of us about ten minutes short of an orgasm and despair hanging over the river like a stinking buzzard, just waiting for us to hold still so it can land.

Virginia does not want to run away with me, anyway. I think the memory of blood spouting out her ankles until her world went dark, from white to hazy to black spots blossoming and blotting out the sight of a red stain spreading up her body toward her head in the tepid water of a Memphis bathtub with lion's feet under it—I think that memory is too fresh and too often repeated for her to go running off into the sunset with a damn gardener, handsome and charming though he might be, without a backward glance or moment of concern that she might fold in on herself again in the worst kind of way.

Then again, she does not cherish her situation at the hospital (who would?), and I have seen her twitch at the mention of my daddy's name. She does not think of me and him in the same mental breath.

I think that I am an experiment for her. She is getting her feet wet again in the world of love. I say again because I have got my suspicions, as I have said. You do not just burst into womanhood knowing how to get down like she does. What she is doing with me is testing the waters. She has got no intention of letting her life slip by between the walls of an insane asylum, surrounded by a bunch of halfwits and maniacs. She is working on getting herself back to fit enough to pass—that is all anyone can hope for, as far as I am concerned—and then she is going to make her exit, with or without anyone else's approval or permission or, for that matter, company.

Of course, this is all conjecture. Who knows what she has got up her sleeve.

She gets me going again with her mouth and climbs right on top of me. I hold on to the steering wheel behind her back and slam my foot down on the fat Cadillac brake pedal. It seems to me that things are moving awfully fast, and I can't see where I am headed. I have got a tit in each eye.

"So tell me some more about your friend Nigel," says Virginia, lying back against the steering wheel, when we have both got to where we were going.

"Be careful, or you'll honk it," I say, indicating the horn behind her shoulder blades.

"Don't worry about that," she says. "Just tell me."

"Tell you what?" I say irritably. This is an annoying turn of conversation; I would as soon talk about something else.

"Anything you know," she says.

"Not much," I say. "We spent a lot of time together when we were little, but I don't know him that well now. He works out at a barbecue place called Paradise and sells me pot. Our mothers died in the same fire. They ran off together."

"Ran off?" she says.

"Yes, that's correct," I say. "It was a torrid affair."

"That's so romantic," says Virginia.

"Maybe so," I say.

"It is," she says.

"Yes."

"But it must have been sad for you," she concedes, and licks my jaw tenderly. "Poor, sad Billy," she says. "No wonder you're so weird."

"I am not so weird," I say.

"It would make anybody weird," she says. "It is nothing to be ashamed of."

"I am not ashamed of anything," I say. She leans back and grasps the edge of the windshield behind her head. The tight shadows of her breasts fall across her rib cage; I press my forehead to the bony hollow of her sternum. She laughs, and I feel the hum of it through the bone of my skull.

"Tell me more about Nigel," she says to the top of my head. She holds it down firmly, crushing my nose and mouth against her. "Why was he running that night?"

"He set a police car on fire," I say.

"Why?"

"I don't know," I say.

"Tell me other things," she says. "You know what I want to hear," she whispers into my trapped ear.

"No, I don't," I say miserably.

"Sure you do," she whispers.

I maintain that I don't, but I am afraid that I do. I wish I were a sexy bandito.

## chapter four

In the heat of the day they stopped to eat, at a truck stop in the desert, under the curious eyes of old men. They must have been a sight: two beautiful women, one black and one white, road dust in their hair and clinging to their skin where the sweat had dried, bone-tired, but lit up from inside. Exhilarated. Smelling like love, high and clear, if you got close.

They ate hamburgers and drank three Nehi sodas apiece from tall, skinny bottles, sucking out of straws with crimps and bends. Every color drink ever made, and they ordered them all at once and then ate some more hamburgers.

"He's coming, Anne," said Carmen, "and he's alone."

"I know," said my mother. "I don't know how on earth he knows which way we went."

"You don't know how we know he's coming, either," said Carmen. They smiled at each other, furtively. They felt very strange. Strange things were happening and had been since the spontaneous simultaneous miraculous orgasm.

"He is, though."

"Reckon so."

My mother took a sip of Nehi, dainty and puckered. "You know what, Carmen," she said. "He's a devil from hell."

"Both of them devils from hell."

"Yes," said my mother. Her eyes narrowed, and she leaned in close. "You reckon we should lay for him?" she said.

Carmen shook her head doubtfully. "I'd just as soon be shut of him," she said. "He'd kill us if he could. We can stay ahead."

"Of course we can," said my mother. She grinned. "I think I could outrun him on foot," she said.

"I ain't felt like this for years," said Carmen. "Not since we were babies."

"Not really babies!" said my mother.

"No, I guess not," laughed Carmen.

When they returned to the car, they found an enormous iguana sunning itself on the hood. The hood was so hot from the engine and the ferocious sun that neither one of them would have dared to put her palm against it. The lizard hissed at them when they approached, flaring dinosaur gills and displaying thousands of needle teeth.

"It's a sight, ain't it?" said one of the old men who was passing by on the way back to his rig. He was an old trucker. He had been driving freight since there were trucks to drive it in.

"Goodness, yes," said my mother.

"You want me to get it off for you, miss?" he asked.

"No, thank you," she said, and took it by its yardlong

tail and flung it far off into the desert, where it landed with a dull thump and scurried away. Carmen watched while the attendant checked the oil and water and filled the car with gas, and my mother ran back to get some more Nehis and ice for the cooler. They were out of peaches, and glad of it.

DAISY HAS TRACKED ME DOWN. She has been calling the house for several days, but Fanny has been cool enough to send her up some cold trails looking for me. Once she saw the Buick cruising up the drive and yelled up to me in time for me to make a sprint for the woods in back.

This time Daisy catches me off-guard. I am trimming around the bases of the oak trees on the drive with the Weed Eater, pretty much hypnotized by the noise, the pleasure of wearing safety goggles, and the magic of vegetation falling away like lard sliced with a curling iron, when I see the blue Buick. It weaves a little bit: a catfish that smells a nice turd or chicken liver floating somewhere nearby, casting about to pinpoint the location. I try to get the oak between me and the car, but it is no use. She probably saw me the second she took the corner. I become too engrossed in yard maintenance for my own good.

There is nothing for it but to shut down the Weed Eater and push the goggles up on my forehead and do the best I can to look pleasantly surprised. I arrange the muscles in my face according to plan, pulling the skin tight in the proper places, wrinkling it in others, baring the teeth of greeting.

It turns out that Daisy is all business. She has got a professional demeanor working for her, that is for sure. She is not going to let any of my nonsense interfere with her plans. She sidles the mass of the Buick up beside me, fat tires folding down the grass on the asphalt's edge in dark stripes. The grass will be fine as long as she does not spin her wheels when she pulls away.

"Well, hello, mister," she says.

"Hi, Daisy," I say.

"You've been so scarce, I started to think I might have to ask one of your friends to escort me at the Rites," she teases.

"They are bad eggs, for the most part," I say.

"I know that much, Billy. That's why I'm dead set on your sweet self," she says. "So are you coming or not?"

"Hell, yes, I'm coming," I say, shifting the grin into shit-eating. "It is just that I have been absorbed in the manifold duties entailed in my work here at the hospital. The cherry trees planted under the supervision of my dear mother have of late been besieged by the attack of a particularly nefarious Norwegian fungus. The fruit are turning into little red raisins before they even have the opportunity to ripen."

"A likely story," she says.

"Truer than Gospel," I say.

"Not much from a heathen," she says. "Speaking of which, my daddy is hot on your trail, too, sonny. He is fixing to make you respectable before he is going to let you show your hide at the ball." This is delivered in fun, but with a little squeeze of warning about the eyes that implies that some violence may be done me if I fail to come around to his way of seeing things: a golf ball accidentally sliced off into the base of my skull from the third tee by the massive force of Mr. Brehard's one wood coming around with three hundred pounds of thick-necked annoyance behind it, my own old man muttering "fore" under his breath as I tumble to my knees. He bends over me: "You feel like working in a cool office yet, boy?" But I am being irrational. These people are not out to get me. They have only my best interest at heart.

"I was just planning to call him, as soon as I went in today," I say. "It's my understanding that he may be able to employ me in some capacity, and make something of me."

"I told him what a clever little feller you are."

"You're as good as gold, Daisy," I say, giving the Weed Eater cord a little tug. It coughs delicately: clearing its throat as if to say to Daisy, ahem. She cools it right off with one of her looks. This conversation is not over yet.

"You better remember it, mister," she says. "Now when are you taking me out to a fancy dinner?"

"On the wages of a laborer?" I protest.

"You can charge it to the Doctor at the club," she says, "though that is pathetic. And you are pathetic. But in a cute way."

"It's true," I say. "I am shiftless. I am the black sheep. I am the prodigal son."

"He had the balls to leave home," she says, with a throaty emphasis on "balls." She is a rough one when you get right down to it, and not so badly versed in the lore of the true church.

"I am he," I say. "I just haven't left yet."

"We'll see," she says. "You just get your handsome self cleaned up and come by for me at seven. And that's not all.

My daddy is expecting you for lunch tomorrow. There will be a discussion of your future." And, it is implied, ours. I am in fear of cringing visibly.

"At your house?" I ask.

She shakes her head. "Downtown," she says. "Be at his office at noon. You all are driving out to the club."

"That's two helpings of roast beef and canned peas in a row," I say.

"Then you can take me somewhere else for dinner," she says, and throws the Buick into gear. The near rear wheel spins, uprooting a patch of grass, and Daisy takes off toward the main building, where she executes a squealing circle in the turnabout. She roars past me on the way out, blowing me a kiss, and trails fluttering fingers backward out her window in a dainty good-bye. I am seized by a paroxysm of trepidation, guilt, regret, and even a small measure of affection as I pull down the goggles from their ridiculous perch on my forehead and yank the Weed Eater to life.

⬤

I cut myself shaving. I have got three little squares of tissue stuck to my jaw when I go by the Brehards' to pick up Daisy for dinner. Mrs. Brehard answers the door. She is a broad woman in a floral-print dress. She has got one of those faces you can never remember when you are not looking at it. Pink and puffy would describe it, I guess. She has got a hairdo without too much color to it one way or another, which moves about as much as a kicker's helmet when she turns her head. You would almost think it has got a chin strap on it.

"You poor thing, you cut yourself," she says. "Daisy will be right down. She is performing her toilet." She says toilet like "twa-lette." I do not know if that is the way you are supposed to say it, but it definitely works for me. I picture Daisy crouched intently over a huge commode.

"That's okay," I say.

"Come on in, and Bethesda will get you a drink," she says. The Brehards are not what you would call niggardly about the dispensation of liquor. That is one of the things I like best about them. "Bethesda!" she yells. "Get Billy Mitchell something cool." I hear Bethesda's voice from somewhere in back.

"That's okay, Mrs. Brehard," I josh. "I've been drinking all day."

"That makes two of us," she says, and an uneasy pause ensues, which I try to fill with a dumb laugh. "Bethesda!" she yells, and cocks her head to the silence. She purses her lips and indicates a straight-backed chair by the door for me to sit in, and stumps off toward the kitchen to get me a drink. I take the moment of privacy that I have been granted to test the wetness of my tissue bandages with a fingertip and slip an exploratory thumb into my left nostril. I yank the thumb out with a start when I hear a heavy tread on the landing at the top of the stairs.

"Oh, it's you," says Mr. Brehard. "I thought you were my wife."

"No sir," I say. "She went to the kitchen."

He is wearing nothing but a pair of briefs that ride way up high on his magnificently corpulent, hairless body, and a pair of navy-blue dress socks. I figure he must have been napping. He does not seem too put out by his marked lack of sartorial splendor; at least, he makes no move to leave. I am saved from my discomfort by Daisy's appearance behind him.

"Get some britches on!" she says, punching him in the back, but all three of us know this is about par for the course. She pats me on the face and goes out the front door.

Mr. Brehard growls down at me, "I hope I'm as proud of you tomorrow as I am right now, boy! I'll see you at noon!" He says that, about being as proud of me tomorrow, each time I pick up Daisy. I cannot imagine what I would have to do to lower myself in Mr. Brehard's esteem.

"Yessir," I say, and holler good-bye to Mrs. Brehard just as she appears from the dark of the hallway with a highball in each hand. I figure she will know what to do with them, and slip back out into the relative safety of twilight. Mr. Brehard's gravelly chuckle chases me like a bronchially afflicted attack dog, but I pull the door to and stop it short.

I have been working hard on the grounds all day, but I do not have an appetite for the dinner I am served at Indian Hills. It is just as I pictured it. The roast beef lies in gray tired folds on one side of my plate, separated by a congealing puddle of gravy from the mashed potatoes and peas. I am starting to feel the same way about this meal every time I order it, but I am unable to make another choice. I would if I could. The fried chicken is good. It is just that I have been ordering the same dinner at the club since I was six years old, and every time I try to make a new choice, "roast beef" comes out of my mouth. I have quit trying to figure it out.

Daisy is putting away the turnip greens like they are going out of style. You can get a good plate of greens at the Indian Hills Country Club. They cook them for about five hours with a ham hock, and all the flavors get friendly, as Huck would say.

"I'll trade you some peas for some greens," I say, but she wags her head no.

"Get your own greens, mister," she says.

She is all talk about the Rites of Dionysius. I am a little nervous that maybe she got to talking to Eunice or Mrs. Klopine and my dress-shopping has been discovered, but she mentions early on that she went to Birmingham to get her gown. She says I am going to like it because it shows off her bosoms. If there is one word I hate, it is "bosom."

Driving her back home, I do not feel entirely myself. I have heard that treachery can be exhilarating; that has not been my experience with it. I feel as though some terrible, irremediable error has been made somewhere along the line. This feeling is not strictly remorse, though I would be a liar if I told myself that was not a part of it. We tongue-kiss in her driveway, and she puts her hand in my lap, but there is no stirring there.

That night after Virginia clambers down her wall, she tells me she has got a craving for barbecue. I figure I know what this is about: She wants to go to Paradise. She has had Nigel on the brain, ever since our encounter on the highway.

"Barbecue, you say," I say.

"That's right," she says.

"Are you my girl, Virginia?" I ask.

"More than you know," she says.

"Well then, all right," I say, even though the roast beef is still sitting kind of heavy. "Let's go to Paradise. They are open at all hours."

"Take me there," she says in a burlesque of breathlessness. "Take me to Paradise."

The lightning bugs are still out and burning up in their brief passion plays of love and rapacity, and the darkling sky is backlit with violet, and I am willing to take her breathlessness for what it would be in the best of all possible worlds. The gloom of dinner has lifted. It is at times like this that I feel a participant in the mystery of life. You never know when a feeling of satisfaction will stumble across you; it can happen at moments of supreme ambivalence. I am caught in an eddy between currents of desire, mine and Virginia's, and possibly Nigel's: whose for whom I am not sure. They crash around one another, and in the center, against all probability, is an eye of quiet, where I am content to lie until I am tossed out.

We roll along, slurping cool beers that foam into our laps, and she murmurs her sarcastic nothings to me, and we take the turn into the trace and tunnel into the darkness. The noises are even louder at night. When the trees close over us, there is no avoiding the feeling that some muscular constrictor might drop heavily and with a mindless violence into the open car from the seething, murmuring canopy above; but far from ruining my little personal moment of peace, the possibility of its ending by reptilian invasion only cements it. I watch Virginia out of the side of my eye as she wonders at the strange turn we have taken, suspicious perhaps that I am leading her to nothing more than an unpeopled hole in the vegetation where I can exorcise my lust under the blanket of an enveloping, ignorant, dispassionate night. With Virginia, I hear the beat of Paradise as if for the first time. We bounce along over the ruts with nothing but the twin ovals of the headlights to guide us into a wall of blackness, and she doubts what she hears at first: the sound of a distant drumming and amplified rhythm.

But there is no denying it. It is James Brown. "I got it!" he yells, as if from inside a lunchbox. The old megaphone speakers are loud, but their fidelity is not all it might be. The branches part and show some sky.

Paradise is a different world at night. The clearing it lies in, which stands so deserted in the day, comes into its own in the dark. By day it is as lonely as a fraternity basement in the morning, when the paper cups and cigarette butts are plastered down in a mud of spilled beer and shoe dirt. At night the clearing is a party. Colored Christmas lights, big old industrial bulbs that sway unnoticed on frayed wires at day, hang in festival loops from the eaves of the pink hut, and a streetlight that stands like a dead tree under the sun comes to life. It lays down a wide circle of light through which silhouettes traverse in familiar talk. Cars drift in from the opposite side of the clearing and lie about in the tall grass without regard for pattern, warm and emanating the smells of gasoline and heated metal. The thick wood behind the clearing is, in reality, only a few hundred yards from the section of Tuscaloosa to which blacks have been gradually shunted by the shoulder of development since it began in earnest in the 1950s.

"Pretty wild," I say to Virginia, indicating the lights. They dodge like shad fry in the wet of her irises.

"You know all about the seamy underbelly, don't you, Billy?" she hisses, and hops out of the car without bothering to open the door. I get a short look up her skirt. I am full of admiration for the fine swing of how she walks up to the window, and how she waves lightly at the row of youths who sit thigh to thigh on the gleaming hood of a dark green Lincoln with suicide doors, which bellies up to the hut like a shark facing into a chummed current. I follow her over to the hole in the pink wall, and poke my head in, expecting to see Nigel, but there is no one in there but a skinny kid of about ten with a round skull adorned with the tiny folded ears of a mole and a close-cropped fuzz of hair. He has a serious demeanor.

"Buddy," I say, "have you seen Nigel Rathberry?" He shakes his head.

"He's big," I say, by way of description.

"I know," he says. "He's my cousin."

"Well," I say, "how about a pint, a loaf, and two Cokes," and then I feel a shadow behind me and Nigel's hand coming to rest on my shoulder.

"Bad Billy," he says.

"Naughty Nigel," I say.

"He giving you trouble, Randy?" Nigel asks the boy. Randy nods yes. "Should I whip his butt?" Randy nods yes again, his somber face finally splitting into a big smile as he puts Cokes on the counter, which is exactly at the level of the top of his cranium.

"You know I'm a black belt," I say.

"I know it," he says. "Bruce Lee giving lessons at the drive-in."

"You remember Virginia," I say. "Nigel Rathberry."

"Whoo," he says.

"Whoo," she says.

"Whoo," I say. "Whoowee." They shake.

"What happened to that biggun?" Nigel asks me, a large arm pulling me away from the hut, nestling me in the crook of his armpit as Virginia leans into the hole and says something to Randy.

"She's making her debut," I say, "and has had done with reprobates like myself."

"I can't blame her," he says. "You need something?"

"Sure," I say. "Virginia wanted some barbecue."

"Un-hunh," he says, as we stroll over toward the Lincoln and the row of cats on the fender.

❦

We pass a bottle from my trunk around on the hood of the Lincoln, and I roll some jays from the bag I get from Nigel, and we have a big time. It is a good night. It seems like everybody's cousins get wind of the fact that we are out there partying and come running for some free liquor, but there is no harm in that. We have a big time.

I imagine, as I fall silent for a moment and loosen my attention from any particularity of focus, that the edges of each of us, the contours that separate us and define each of us as individuals in relation to one another, have gone soft. That is what can happen to you at Paradise (or anywhere, for that matter) if you will allow yourself to become part of a collective moment.

That is why I am drawn to Paradise, to the warmth and color that live secretly out in the dark of the Alabama jungle. Paradise has no structure; the moments when the self can dissolve come of their own volition, flapping across time like great lumbering bats, and suddenly overtake you. Of course there are the drugs, and of course there is the liquor and the groove of the pink hut that never stops. But those are ancillary to the true phenomenon. There is in the place and in the darkness of it, the darkness that lingers like a smell even in daylight, an immanent invitation to abandonment.

"You feel fine, don't you, Billy?" says Nigel. I am wasted and happy, lodged between two of his friends on the hood of the Lincoln. Their shoulders squeeze and brush against me with fraternal weight. A kid at the end, someone's younger brother, keeps getting pushed off the front of the hood and climbing back on with mild complaint, but he is pleased just to be there; he smiles shyly each time his ass reaches the point of no return. Someone has put on a lot of Burma Shave.

"Yes, I feel fine," I say. "Things are very fine."

"That's a good feeling, isn't it?" Nigel says. "I wish I were feeling that way."

"Yes, I wish you were, too," I say.

"It's the only way to feel!" says Mark, the one to my left.

"Yes," I say.

"I have been meaning to ask you something," says Nigel. "You remember that night you all picked me up." The air does not change; the kid slides off and climbs aboard.

"You burnt up a car," I say.

"Yeah, I did," he says. "Why was the Doctor with the sheriff in that car that came after us?"

"He was playing poker at the station," I say.

"Is that right."

"Yes, that's what he told me. I think he knew it was you in the convertible, but he was not sure it was mine."

"Is the Doctor a political man?" asks Nigel.

"I believe he votes Democrat," I say, which prompts smiles all round. Virginia, across the lot, swings Randy around by his armpits, and dips him in the circle of clarity cast by the streetlight.

"Votes Democrat, I like that," says Nigel. He lights another joint, and sends it, by way of me, down the length of the hood. I toke hard, and hold my breath. There is a bloom of black, and I let it out, to find that Nigel is even closer; he stands pressed against my knees, and leans in to me.

"Billy," he says, "why do you come here and hang around?"

"I like it, that's all," I say.

"You like it."

I am at a loss for words. "I feel an affinity," I say.

"A what?"

"A connection. It's kind of a weird time to talk about it," I say, indicating our company.

"Connection to what?" he asks incredulously.

"Well, I guess to you," I say. "I have tried to explain."

"How we are like brothers."

"You remember. I am surprised."

"I think perhaps you should expand on that now," says Nigel.

"That's not my thing now. I never really worked it out," I admit. "I have been having visions."

"Religious visions or some shit?"

"No, no," I say. "I see Carmen and Anne in dreams. The Doctor is chasing them. He is acting like a lunatic. I believe I am coming to an understanding." Nigel shakes his head.

"You are out to a long lunch, Billy," he says.

"Probably so," I agree.

"You'd be best to put all that behind you," he says. "That shit is over. This is a new time." I shift on the hood and open another beer. My hands feel funny, as though they are not my own, and fumble with the tab after I pull it off. I want no part of his new time.

"Are you listening to me?" says Nigel. "This is a new time. I haven't seen Antoine."

"Who is Antoine?" I ask.

"The dude on the motorcycle," he says.

"He was probably afraid to see you again," I say.

"Man, nobody has seen him," says Nigel. "He is just gone."

"I'll bet he went to Florida," I say. "That's what I would do if you were after me."

"You got to figure out where you stand before you come around here again," says Nigel. "I hope I am making myself clear. Think hard before you get involved." Is he menacing me, or offering advice? I do not know. I cannot read his face.

"They never caught him," I say. "You're talking shit. We have to go." Virginia spins in the light, with Randy on her back, a dizzy whirl apart from us. I call out to Virginia. She staggers over, spun off course by the panic in her inner ear. Randy's chin rests on her shoulder. They are both glazed and hilarious with the difficulty of focusing.

"We've got to go," I say.

"The party just started," she says, though we on the Lincoln are about all that is left of it. Randy's nimble little hands grope about on her face. She squints against their grip.

"You all stay out of trouble," says Nigel.

"Nigel, you stay out of trouble," I say, and he shakes his head.

"Way too late for that," he says.

"I will come back and talk to you," I say.

"Do what you have to, Billy," he says, and takes Randy off of Virginia's back. The little boy climbs on him like he is a tree, and perches on his shoulders, hands buried past the wrist in Nigel's dome of hair.

I reach into my pocket and toy with my keys. " 'Bye, Nigel," says Virginia, with no hint of suggestion. She is beyond me, that is for sure. "I am sorry we did not get to chat more. We'll come again. Good-bye you all," she says to the rest.

"Yeah, okay," Nigel says absently, moving Randy's feet in circles, as if they are on the pedals of a bicycle.

"I'm going to collect myself. I can explain everything," I say: meaning, everything: the memories, the reason Nigel looms so tall in my symbolic life, his error in assuming that the mysterious Antoine is dead, if in fact that is what he assumes.

"You are drunk as a dog," he says.

"That's correct," I say.

"I've got big news for you, son," Virginia says. It is on the road home all bright-faced and wasted in the dashboard light and light of the moon.

"I have got some heavy things on my mind, Virginia," I say.

"Big news, and you ain't going to hear it until we are on the beach," she says.

"Is it good news or bad news?" I ask.

"That all depends," she says, "on whether or not you drive to the beach."

"The river," I say.

"The real beach," she says, "on the ocean."

What she is talking about is not getting her back in the sack before the nurse comes in at dawn to drain Louise, which is to say: What she is talking about is leaving hanging the spotted sheet of our union, in the form of a rope ladder. A decision is demanded of me; I am at a juncture. If I say no to Virginia, who is to say how it will go with us? But if I say yes:

If I say yes, I will have violated one of my primary principles: I will have made a decision that runs directly into the face of my plan to live the life of least resistance. There is no denying that busting a lunatic out of her bin and heading for the beach is going to turn some heads. I have no doubt that the police would be on the lookout for Virginia. Though she, of course, poses no threat to anyone but herself, there are a few dangerous inmates at Branson. But the intervention of the police, in reality, is the least of my worries. The ladder left flapping for all to see in the morning would scream out my defection from normal life in dangling, ropy semaphore: defection from my father, defection from Daisy, defection from my post as head groundsman. There is no return if I head for the beach.

I suggest that an hour by the river might leave us just as sated, but she is having none of it. I am fooling neither of us.

"If you do not take me to the ocean," she says, "I am through with you." And that is all there is to it. I guess I am hoist by my own damn petard. There is nothing to do but to stop in the next county south and buy whiskey, and slide on down the highway. Gulf Shores is not more than six hours from Tuscaloosa in the daytime, and at night you can go as fast as you like as drunk as you like. There is no one to stop you.

It would seem that a decision of such an irrevocable nature would sing through you like the soul of all courage. That is not the way it happens with me. We drive toward the water, Virginia lying on her back with her head pillowed on my thigh, and I try to get a taste of triumph in the air, leaning my head out the side and squinting straight into the wind until my tongue goes dry and tears stream back toward my ears, but it is of no use. I feel nothing but drunker and deader. Our skins go numb from the buffeting of the wind. Dawn is coming fast, and I have put one hundred miles behind us, and I think to myself, if this is freedom, well fuck it. And that is before Virginia decides to break down seventy miles short of the coast and tell me her big secret.

"Actually, there are two secrets," she says. "Which one do you want first?"

"The first one," I say.

"I'm going to tell you the second one first," she says.

"Tell me the second one."

"Your daddy is onto us," she says.

"I was afraid of that," I say.

"I mean he is definitely onto us."

"Definitely."

"Definitely. He come up to the ward this evening and had me taken out of the room with Louise."

"The catatonic."

"The very one. And had me put back in my old room and told the nurse to keep an eye on me and that I was a subversive element."

"So how did you get here?"

"I clumped her one."

"Excuse me?"

"I clumped her one on the head," she says.

"With what?" I ask. Clumping items are in short supply on the wards at Branson.

"With mine," she says.

"Your head."

"Yeah, boy. I got Darleeta to start squalling like she was having a seizure or something, and then Nurse Bickerty come in, and I gave her what for."

"Are you okay?" I ask, feeling around at her head in the dark. "What about Nurse Bickerty?"

"She's fine. I tied her up and gagged her with some strips

of sheet and put her in my bed. Darleeta is taking care of her."

The first secret, she goes on to tell me, is that my sorry seed has taken root in her.

"I am overjoyed," I say. This is not strictly true, but I find that discovering that you are going to be a father will make you reel for a moment: That is a fact. But somehow you have a hard time reconciling it with what you know to be true, which is to say the plastic of the steering wheel getting greasy under your palm, and the rainy smell of wet asphalt steaming around you, mixed in with the burning breath of a long drunk. There is a piece of you, real as a flank steak, swelling like a cancer in someone else's belly, but your mind cannot get a purchase on it. I cannot but feel that I am unprepared. It seems that my life, which I have attempted, with a few concessions to my id, to keep free of trouble, has become a confluence of ill winds.

Morning finds us in the parking lot of the new Shoney's in Gulf Shores. Shoney stands defiantly cheerful in the empty lot, offering up his gargantuan plastic hamburger to the heavens, where gulls wheel and keen in the gray. The salt in the breeze coming off the Gulf leaves the skin inside my elbows and behind my knees slightly sticky. In fact, I am pretty much glued to the leather. Virginia's hair (grown longer now—I have known her long enough to see her hair grow!) lies lank and cleaves to her face beside her nose and mouth, where she has just wiped away the last strands of thin vomit. I imagine that there is some of her vomit on the outside of the passenger door, as well, but she has done a good job of keeping it out of the interior. There is nothing worse than driving around in a car full of puke, even if the top is down.

"Honey, we need to talk," I say. She spits and looks off to sea. An ancient couple creak spryly along the boardwalk across the street, where the levy we are parked on fades off into sand and tidal flats. The woman holds the man under his arm in the traditional gesture of escort, but it is apparent from the slight yaw in their progress that he is leaning upon her for support. "I mean, if we don't go back," I say, "and don't misunderstand me—I don't want to go back—we have to go somewhere. I need to find a job."

"You cocksucker," she says. "You want to go back."

"Virginia, I can't go back," I say. "Not that I would if I could."

"I'm not going back," she says. "I got what I came with, and I'm getting out. You do whatever you want."

"Came with?" I say. "You came with nothing."

"That's all you know, you faithless asshole," she says. She is lost in some kind of paranoid despair, but she is trying to pass it off as cryptic drunkenness and indifference. She puts a Camel between her cracked lips and takes it out again, picking a shred of tobacco off her tongue with thumb and index finger. She looks at it like it is a maggot she found in her lunch meat, and lights the cigarette.

"Billy, you're such a turd," she tells me. "You think you are brilliant and dispassionate, but you are a turd."

"Often shyness is mistaken for arrogance," I say.

"Oh, please," she says. "You think acting like a retard most of the time is a perfect camouflage for a visionary of your stature."

I can tell she is just getting warmed up. "I beg you not to harangue me," I say. "I do not feel too well."

"You will shut up," she says, and pauses to take a huge drag on her smoke, holding up a finger to forestall any objection or confession I might have to offer. I can almost hear the crackle of ignition as the ash lengthens alarmingly toward her lips. But all she says is, "This is real. You got to get off your sad ass now. You can cut that dreamy, inscrutable shit out."

I figure I am due a smoke myself and shake one out of the pack that lies between us on the leather. My possible future wife has got me up against the barbed wire. It is the inscrutability comment that has really got me uncomfortable. It seems that my work in that direction has been of little avail.

"Those are mighty hard words," I say.

"And that," she says. "Don't you do that. Don't you retreat into idiom like you think I don't know you think that's funny. You smug fuck."

"Retreat into idiom?" I say.

She says, "Idiom, you shit, idiom! You think you're the only one who speaks English?"

I can tell she is really pissed at me. It is not just what she is saying. It is the fact that she is willing to say it. That is one thing you will learn if you watch carefully: People hold on to the truth, or what they see to be the truth, as if it is some final secret hostage they don't even want you to know they have got until they figure they can make use of it. It looks to me like Virginia has had this one cooling off for a while.

"Are you sure you are pregnant?" I ask. She takes my hand tenderly and brings it to her lips as though to kiss it and bites my index finger so hard I hear the crunch of bone behind the first joint.

"Sorry," she says. It is bent at the middle, and where her teeth bore down, it looks to be swelling into a fleshy walnut. The tip is turning purple-black.

But to not worry about her getting pregnant: Now what can she possibly have meant by that, if she is indeed carrying the fruit of my loins within her? I took it to mean that she was as barren as a battlefield, despite the apparent ripeness—fecundity even—that she practically stank with when she came around that corner of my house and stood in the flower bed in her bare feet.

"Baby," I say, "I thought you said you couldn't."

Clearly that was not the most tactful thing to say, but my finger hurts like hell, and that is the first thing that comes to mind. Strangely, she does not light into me. "I never thought it could happen," she says.

"Ah," I say. "Like dying."

"No," she says, "I mean I never thought it could happen again. I was pregnant when I came, but I never thought it could happen again." She is just looking off at the water. It is coming in fast, covering the marsh grasses and sandbars so that you can't see it happen if you watch, but if you look away and then look back, you will see that the stalks have grown shorter and the patches of land have grown smaller and more desperately far from one another. "They took it right out of me first thing," she says. "I thought they fixed me afterward."

"Lordy," I say, "they don't do that kind of thing, Virginia."

"They don't do that kind of thing? They don't do that kind of thing? What the fuck are you talking about!" she yells. "Why do you think I got shut up? I was pregnant with a black man's baby, and my psychotic father tied me up and brought me to Tuscaloosa."

"I thought you tried to kill yourself," I say. "Your ankles, I mean."

"You are so fucking dumb. That was six years ago. He just freshened them up some."

"Jesus."

"I came in, they laid me down on a table and gave me gas, and I woke up empty. Maybe it was a relief, I don't know, to sit still for a while. I didn't talk for five days. But I aim to keep this one. It's mine!" she yells. "Mine! I ain't going back." She is not going to break down, either. I have not known her to cry.

"You were in love," I say.

"What do you know?" she says. "You think it all comes back to you. It has nothing to do with you."

Now what can you say to an answer like that?

"Is this one going to be pink?" I ask.

"You'll just have to see," she says. And I guess I will.

I guess I will, though as Virginia turns away and pukes again, memory and imagination overtake one another and play out for me a terrible masque:

Of course Nigel was there with me. I know it was summertime, but I cannot remember what summer it was. Perhaps the summer between grade school and junior high, or between junior high and high school. It may be that memory serves me ill, and it was no significant summer at all; it could have been any summer when I was still soft and hairless. It may be that the force of constant return (this is not my first return to the site, or the second, or fifth or tenth, no: not even close) has resulted in the filmic quality of the memory. I can play it back as I please: slowly, now quickly, freezing on a frame. I reverse the roles of characters, bring in new ones when the original cast refuses to titillate, cooperate. And thank goodness it is so. This particular memory was and re mains the root of my imaginative life, a central series of images to which all others turn for reference. I guess it is a good one. It is definitely an unusual one. It is a hard event to explain away.

We were out back of the hospital in the woods, the two of us having cut out of our respective roles as Octopus-level Indian Hills Swim Team Member and assistant flower-bed weeder. It was hot as hell, and I had a heat rash. I was always getting heat rash, especially when I was spending a lot of time running around in the woods, as I was in those days. I was at that weird age where I was spending as much time as possible locked up in the bathroom upstairs or out in the woods in back of the hospital. Though the bathroom was more comfortable and had a lock on it, there was the risk of being found out and ridiculed by Fanny, who was always around the house somewhere. So the woods were actually more private. There was not much going on out there. I usually had them pretty much to myself.

So my surprise was considerable when Nigel pointed out the naked lady. We had just lit up a couple of the Doctor's Pall Malls, walking along kicking at roots, when his eyes bugged out, and he caught me by the arm. Mine must have bugged out, too. Until that time, my experience with naked ladies was pretty much negligible. I had not even had the normal glimpses of my mother getting in and out of the bathtub and that kind of thing. The Doctor did his gallivanting elsewhere. She was facing away from us, and we hit the deck in a hurry.

She was sitting down on the leaf-covered dirt with her left arm thrown out straight behind her, supporting her weight, and her right shoulder hunched forward, rolling around in its socket. Fantasy has made her lovely, but in truth she was just a normal woman, in her thirties, thick-waisted and drop-shouldered with a heavier than normal head, and fresh earth ground into the dimpled fold behind her elbow. It sounds funny. But for some reason, there was nothing funny about it, and she turned around over the thrown-back shoulder and looked right at us where we lay side by side on our stomachs, ground-out cigarettes clenched in our fists, spiky erections digging into the soil, and she did not laugh either. Nor did she evince any surprise. She was no more amazed or ashamed by our presence than a dog might have been had we stumbled upon it licking its balls in a clearing. She swiveled her body around on the fulcrum of one soft white buttock and faced us splay-legged with a fist tightly curled in her genital crevice.

"Pardon us," I said. Nigel's eyes were flying all over the woods. She had her mouth a little bit open, and her tongue looked slightly swollen, as though it were trying to escape the bounds of her head. "We didn't know you were here," I said.

I think she responded, "Satyrs in the glade," but there is no telling. I'll bet I did not know what a satyr was back then; and besides, your memory can play tricks on you.

"We should fuck her," I said to Nigel.

"Nah," he said, "you do it."

"Ma'am," I said, "do you understand us?" She did not say a thing, just kept moving her fist in that circle. "See, she doesn't mind," I said. "She wants us to. You can go first."

"You go first," he said. We were on our knees now, facing her, and we were bound by the complicity of any two men or boys who have seen one another's excitement. I reached over for his belt buckle and undid it. His hands, unsure of finding a safe place to light, fluttered like dark birds around his hips.

"You go," I said, tugging at his waistband. When she saw his penis emerge, she took her fist from her lap and put that hand behind her with the other. There was no desire on her face; nor was there any fear, or excitement, or anything. She made room for him by lying back, and I knelt a few feet from them, watching the narrow bulbs of Nigel's butt rise and contract over the white expanse of her. He finished, eyes ahead as if in a sprint at the end, and rolled off, hurriedly kicking and tugging his pants up from his ankles, where they had been the whole time. She put her fist back as though it had never happened, and lay looking up through the pines at the sky.

"Now you go," said Nigel.

"I don't feel like it," I said.

"Chicken," he said, and I said no, that wasn't it. I mean, that may have been a part of it. But I think that in some measure I was right, that there was something else at play. It was not that the desire went out of me. My little cock was so hard it hurt, and my head spun. I relit one of the crunched-out Pall Malls and handed it to Nigel.

"She liked it," I said, and he nodded.

"Yeah," he said. "Do you think she's going to tell?"

"They wouldn't believe her," I said. We left her there in the dirt. She was not put out in the least bit. It does not sound like a charitable thing, but what else was there to do? I even said " 'Bye" and gave her a little wave, but I don't think she saw it. We walked back to the outskirts of the lawn, where we peered out from a bed of chrysanthemums. We smoked a few more smokes and felt sick after a while and went back to the rear of my house to get some lemonade out of Fanny.

Caesar was standing on the porch with his hat in one hand and his handkerchief in the other. He kept wiping at his bulbous forehead with the handkerchief. He was a frightening figure to me and seemed somehow terribly out of place no matter where he was. He appeared that way that afternoon. I wish I could put better words to it, but I can describe it no more specifically than this: It was as if he possessed a horrible awareness of something, some grim and savage fact he could never speak, but that threatened to burst out of the starched confines of his tight collars and explode in sanguineous rage.

"What have you seen?" he said, and Nigel said, "Nothing," and it was another scene like after I killed the goat. They got into the car without any more talk and drove away. I have no idea what Caesar knew, or what Nigel told him. Fanny wouldn't give me anything in particular when I tried to milk a little information out of her, only that one of the lunatics had been found naked in the woods. It was not an everyday occurrence, but nothing to get excited about.

I was afraid for a while that Nigel might let on what had happened. I had visions of terrible tortures in the Rathberry home, of Caesar's fury finally let loose inside the mysterious gloom of their house by the river, of beating and even burning. I was probably a little carried away in my imaginings. I was afraid that if Caesar found out, he would tell the Doctor, and my part in the episode would be revealed. However, the Doctor never found out. At least, I never heard tell of it if he did. But I am certain: He did not.

*chapter five*

The Doctor must have been on the second dog by the time he got to the old man with the card table. He had not taken the engine heat into account; it was likely to cook the lead dog from the stomach upward. Ten miles out, the first hound had started looking back around at him, still yelling fit to bust but with a distracted expression on its long face, as though something had happened to the back end of it that confused the business of the front end. No use in a baked hound. No blankets in the trunk, either, to wrap the dog in. He took off his clothes and swaddled the dog in them, dressed it up in his very own clothes, and tied it back on. He was driving in nothing but his boxer shorts and his hunting boots.

He probably changed hounds each time he filled his tank, took the used one and threw it in the back, where it shook and foamed from the strain of its weird chase, dead bugs in its fangs, eyes in dried-out slits, but no less enthused, still croaking. He stripped it and put a fresh one in the clothes, and strapped it up just like the first. It was trying to get loose and run out ahead of the car, which was moving an easy eighty miles an hour, the hound's long ears and his starchy shirtsleeves cracking back at the windshield in the breeze. He stole a bucket from one of the gas stations and filled it each time he stopped, watering the nearly dead dog and the one that hadn't got strapped up yet and was going hoarse from its yelling.

When they passed the peach stand, the lead dog reared its head straight up and moaned, its lips pursed just like a person's. It was howling, which is how you know you have got what you are looking for treed; or at least the dog thinks so. He skidded off the highway and tore back to where the old farmer was sitting. Still plenty of peaches for sale. The Doctor got out. The dog was looking right at the old man, howling its heart out, still trying to wriggle free, but the Doctor had it trussed good. The Doctor was a man who knew his knots. The two in the car were squashed up against the windows.

"Hidy," said the farmer. "It's hot, ain't it," he said, looking at the Doctor's outfit.

"It's hot," said the Doctor. "You seen a white woman with a colored girl come through here?"

"Yessir, I did. Hit were in the morning. Done bought four baskets of them peaches."

"Headed west?"

"Yep," said the farmer.

"How long ago?"

The farmer looked up at the sun. "Few hours, I reckon," he said.

"Much obliged," said the Doctor, and got back into the car. The old man was calling something to him, but he couldn't hear over the dogs.

"What's that?" asked the Doctor.

"Them's blueticks, ain't they?" said the old man.

"That's right," said the Doctor.

"Them's a good breed, I reckon. I had me one of them oncet." He nodded. "You'll get em," he said. The Doctor waved and jammed his car into gear, grinding up until he was at the top of his third, and disappeared from the farmer's sight.

At the truck stop the last dog reared up and howled treed. The other two escaped when the Doctor got out, and he ran behind them to the back side of the building, where they had the iguana cornered in a mess of oil drums. He ran back to the car and got his gun and blew the lizard clean in half, and threw the dogs back in the car. The waitress told him he was an hour back from my mother and Carmen Rathberry.

IT IS NO MILD thought to think: that your father who is a stranger to you has had his hands inside your lover, and has somewhere in a hardwood cabinet the secrets of her life and illness.

In time Virginia goes to sleep, her head lying perhaps uncomfortably against the door. I place the cushion of my shirt beneath her head; her eyelids flutter as I gently cradle the dead weight of her head and slip the oxford under. I am right to do it, I note, as the thin-furred rubber lips of the window seal have dug a red crease into her cheek. If I could, I would sleep as well, but I am troubled by the ghosts of my future. As the liquor evaporates out of me and the cigarettes burn to butts one by one, the lot slowly fills with the sad, softly creeping vehicles of the elderly, and the sun, risen fully, burns a wan circle in the muggy cover of cloud. My hand hurts like a new kind of pain.

The elderly know in their brittle hollow bones, as migratory birds know the exact locations of sheltered coves in Costa Rica, where to get the cheapest breakfasts. I do not know when I picked up the awareness of this phenomenon, but it is a certainty. You have only to follow the cautious Chryslers

and Plymouths down any road at dawn to find the least ex-
pensive square meal available in a given locale. It looks to me
like Shoney's has got a breakfast buffet going strong, and I
know I can get some ice in there.

There have been times in my life when all I needed to set
things to rights was a square meal; aware that this is probably
not one of those times, I nevertheless decide that some eggs
and coffee will do me no harm in any event and walk across
the lot. The asphalt seems too warm for the time of day;
maybe I have been in the car longer than I imagined. Or
perhaps the magma below is pooling itself for an upward surge
against the thin crust, and Virginia and I and Shoney and the
geriatric brigade are all to be thrown skyward and then sucked
down and disintegrated in small hissing pops, like spit on a
griddle. You never can tell. I tread lightly.

The hostess behind the smoked-glass door points sternly to
three icons that have been pasted to the inside of the window:
a bare chest without nipples and bare feet and a dog, each
centered in a slashed red circle, and I realize dimly that I am
neither shod nor shirted. I wave to her in cooperative understanding, eager not to incur her disapproval (for the hos-
tility of strangers, at this point, is more than I can bear), and
pad back to the car. It seems a crime to take the shirt from
under Virginia's head; in light of the slight betrayal that I have
planned, I cannot take the shirt. I reach down under the ac-
celerator and get my Weejuns, and recall that her smock is in
the trunk along with her pajama britches. I pop the trunk and
try it on for size and head back to Shoney's, flapping like a
sage. Once inside, I find that I can stomach nothing but balls
of honeydew. I eat a plate of them, weird sweet balls of water,

and take a coffee and a dishrag full of ice for the road.

Sadly, there are things to which I must attend before I leave Tuscaloosa for good. I ease the Eldo into gear and nose my way back to the highway. Virginia is breathing regularly, and I am not worried about her at all and feel one moment of hope for us, for the three of us, as we crest the arc of the bridge that connects Gulf Shores to the mainland and I can see across the flats to where the earth curves away. The top of the bridge is higher than anything in Gulf Shores except for the tallest waterslide at Gatorland and the Ferris wheel in the itinerant fair that comes every summer for three weeks, which is reputed to be the sixth largest in the world.

Papa's will do for a place to hide Virginia while I attend to my business. I imagine they will get on well. I can picture it: They will sit together on folding chairs in the dirt in front of the trailer, chawing big hunks of plug and spitting at the balding rooster. Virginia is still sleeping like the dead as I blow through late-morning Tuscaloosa hunkered down low in the seat, with my mirrored shades protecting me from the eyes of judgment. She did not even wake when I stopped to get gas. My awareness has become airy and attenuated from lack of sleep, and fearful visions flit across the screen of my psyche, but I pay them no heed and keep the pedal down, heading upriver, heading for Peterson.

Virginia wakes at the change to quiet as I decelerate and turn off the road onto the gravel at the base of Papa's driveway.

"Where we at?" she asks me sleepily.

"This is my grandfather's place," I say. "You can stay here until tonight. There are some things I have to set straight before I leave town."

"Cowboy settles his debts," she says. The sun, while she was sleeping, colored her on one side of her face. An unspeakable tenderness seizes me at the sight of this asymmetry of pink and white; I reach over and gently poke the burned side of her forehead. When I remove my finger, the spot where it touched is pale and softly blushes red again.

"What," she says, and raises her palm to where I touched her.

"Nothing. Got me a showdown," I say, getting out and stretching a little bit. I cannot explain the complexity of my feeling. I move to the trailer and knock on the frame of the screen door.

"Who the fuck that?" yells Papa.

"It's me," I yell back, and the inside door swings away. Everybody I talk to is in his underwear.

"Hey, boy," he says, and, peering, "Who that in the car?"

"She's a lunatic," I say. "I knocked her up, and we're running away to California. Can she stay here for a day?"

He raises a palm in greeting to her. She waves back sunnily. "I reckon," he says, "if you willing to vouch for her good character."

"Oh, she's a gem, Papa."

"Well," he says. "What you done to your finger?"

"I slammed it in the door," I say.

"Look like a damn plumb," he says. "What you need is some medical attention."

"You got any?" I ask. He nods and turns away into the cave of his trailer, leaving the door agape.

"He said fine," I call to Virginia, and she looks pleased enough. I figured she would be mad when she woke up in spitting distance of the hospital, but of course there is no telling.

"Of course he did," she says. She is looking over at the run, where the hounds are pressed against the chicken wire so hard it looks like their heads might pass through it in hexagonal tubes of meat. She strolls over and squats next to the enclosure, putting her fingers through to be licked and snotted and sucked. Some people will tell you that a hound dog is no good because it is so dumb and single-minded. These are the aspects of the hound character that I most admire. A hound is not prone to wasting days considering the course of right action. A hound operates purely on instinct and has got commitment to its cause.

Papa comes back out with a short stack of Dixie cups, an ice tray, and half a fifth of bourbon, and pants on. He sets the fixings on the dusty hood of the Corvette and cracks the ice apart. He puts a cube in each of three cups.

"I'm not having any," says Virginia. "I'm fixing to have a baby." That had not occurred to me. It is a good thing I am not pregnant. The last thing this child needs on top of a crazy mother and me for a father is a waterlogged brain.

"Could you use some lemonade, miss?" asks Papa with uncharacteristic consideration. To him, it is as though someone were taking extra good care to feed his bluetick puppies right when he was laid up with jaundice.

"I reckon I could," says Virginia, "if it is no trouble, Mr. Mitchell. And please call me Virginia."

"Ain't no trouble," he says, and practically crabscampers back to the trailer. I get some of the ice in the soggy rag and put it on my finger. I swear to God I can feel every pump of my heart from my fingertip all the way to my brainpan. He reemerges not with a glass of lemonade, but with a lemon, a bag of sugar, and a Mason jar cradled in his arms, and an open buck knife clenched in his teeth. He comes back over and gets to work cutting and squeezing and stirring. They are going to get on all right. "Them's fine dogs, ain't they?" he says to Virginia, who is still over there getting licked on.

"Gorgeous," she says.

"You all will be okay until I get back," I say. I go over to where Virginia squats and whisper in her ear that I love her. "If he gets too drunk or mean, just ask him why they call him the Possum," I tell her. "He'll still be telling it when I get back."

"Don't you touch that bitch," says Virginia, under her breath.

"I am not fixing to," I say, and get back in the car, where the seat is still slick from the sweat of my back. They wave me off down the dusty, treeless drive. It does not look like I am going to be quite on time for my meeting with Mr. Brehard, and I am not looking my best. One glance in the rearview mirror tells me that. But so it goes. I am not an aspiring newspaperman.

Virginia is correct in her assumption that I intend to speak with Daisy, in person if possible. A sense of obligation remains, even in the face of these strange circumstances and the decision I have made to leave with Virginia. It is a funny thing, that the dictates of conventional decency will remain with you in a time of crisis. I would like to think that I am essentially a decent person, and that that is the reason I feel I must have these final meetings, but that is not the whole story; if I were really decent, they would not be necessary. I would have tactfully ended my relationship with Daisy weeks ago, perhaps months ago. I believe that even at this late date I am driven by a need to appear decent, which is quite different from a need to actually be decent. It is an old story with southern men, and you would think that once you have seen the actual truth of it, you could let convention slide. But that is not the way it works, unfortunately. Adherence to the conventions of honor is what I am about, rather than adherence to an actual code. I am going to take my beating for my own sake; dishing it out will probably not bring any comfort to Daisy, but taking it will give me some measure of masochistic satisfaction.

But Daisy is the lesser of my two personal worries. My father, of course, is the greater worry. Should I be afraid of him, or should I despise him? And can I forget that he is my father, after all: That, of course, is the real question. In what fashion do we owe one another, if at all, and can there be, at the core of the rotten mess that is the two of us, father and son, any love left?

I need to know these things, but I am not willing for an

instant to sacrifice my chance with Virginia for them. Under no circumstance will I allow the Doctor to know where she is: Of that, at least, I am certain. Without question, our meeting will be a strange one, for I plan to explain my revelations to him in detail: the story of the lovers, the chase, and the final annihilation. I wonder if the Doctor will dispute my version of history; after all, I have no evidence, and no hope of any.

But in the end, in this case, I am in no search of proof. My need for Virginia is enough. Whether my dreams are true is of no practical importance in terms of changing my mind about leaving, but how sweet and how bitter it would be to have the Doctor's admission of guilt, to make my leaving clean, and to free my hind foot from where it is caught in the fold of memory, forever tugging me back.

I wonder if there is any chance of forgiveness, one way or another: if he is altogether a demon, or if he is a man who was goaded by a broken heart to an unspeakable act: if there is any difference: if he is a lunatic: or if I am.

Metaphysical concerns aside, there is the matter of getting my hands on a few cash dollars with which to effect our escape. I have got some ideas cooking on this score. I can get my hands on a few hundred at home: the summer's wages, paid in cash by the Doctor himself, sitting in a drawer in my bureau. In the bureau there is also a piece of paper that was worth a thousand dollars at the time of my mother's death, which may have appreciated a bit in the interim. It is some kind of savings bond; I am not sure exactly what, but I will work that out at my leisure later on.

I figure I will invest some of the cash in a grocery bag of dope from Nigel, if there is time on the way out. Either he has some kind of rotating harvest going, or he really put some by last fall; one way or another, he is not short on product. It should not be hard to unload at a handsome profit on the hippies in Berkeley or Los Angeles and will get us in on the radical movement. From what I hear, you are nobody out there if you are not in on the radical movement, and it would be irresponsible to neglect the financial aspect of raising a family of my own. I have a feeling the Doctor is not going to help me along much, and I hope fervently that Virginia's family never ferrets us out. They sound like nothing but trouble.

Downtown smells of asphalt and the excretory breath of the papermill. I nuzzle up to the curb in front of Brehard's office building, which is low-slung and made out of brick, with black windows. Taupe-painted air conditioners, big as television consoles, suck to the walls at intervals like swollen steely ticks and emit a machined hum and hot breath. The name of the enterprise, *The Tuscaloosa Standard*, stands in white-lettered relief two inches off the brick above the entrance. It is an unprepossessing building of the sort that a sinister government office might occupy, with the requisite number of anonymous shit-colored sedans lined up out front.

The office is sparsely populated, and I see immediately that the sagging leather chair in Brehard's glass booth at the back is empty. There is a wilted receptionist up front, and behind her a handful of men who look like they might sell insurance or real estate sit before typewriters and telephones in their shirtsleeves. A couple of them say, "Hey, Billy," and I nod cordially to them.

"How you all doing?" I say. They trade some funny looks with each other.

"Not bad," says one, named Fishly Baker.

"All right then, Fishly," I say.

"Say, Billy," says Fishly, "there's some people looking for you."

"Yeah, I figured so," I say. "I am late for my appointment."

"Appointment, shit," he says. "Ain't no appointments today. Have you heard the news?" All the others turn their heads down but cock their ears.

"What news is that?" I say warily. I figured the Doctor would be mad, but I did not think he would report us missing.

"Somebody done blown up Pete Hobson's office," he says, and I think, oh Christ, my father is dead, too. But the men around me are not reverent enough in their silence for that to be so. They are curious, rather than solemn.

"Anyone hurt?" I ask.

"Not bad," says Fishly. "One of them deputies got his arm cut up some, but he's going to be all right. They're getting some dogs to go sniffing around. Hobson says it's one of them crazy niggers for sure. It's been one hell of a morning."

"Damn," I say.

Fishly nods and puts a foot up on a chair, and his elbow on that knee. It is an abbreviated, indoor version of the conversational squat. He has the stub of a pencil behind his right ear, and the top button of his shirt is undone beneath his loosened tie; he is well on the way to acquiring the proper mannerisms of a journeyman reporter.

"Say, Billy, on an unrelated note," says Fishly.

"Yeah?"

"You know anything about one of your lunatics busting out?"

"That ain't news, Fishly," I say, faking a smile.

"I guess not," he says. "I guess we got our hands full for one day, all right."

"I should say. But, Fishly," I say, "would you give Mr. Brehard a message for me?"

"I sure would, Billy," he says.

"You tell him I have found some other employment out of town. I will be leaving for a while."

"Hell, you can tell him yourself," he says. "He's right down the block eating lunch with Daisy at Candyland."

"All right," I say. "May I make a phone call?" He nods and points me to the chair at his own desk.

"Go right ahead," he says. I dial up home, and Fanny answers after three rings.

"It's me," I say.

"The Doctor almost got blown up," she says.

"I heard that," I say. "I am down at the *Standard.*"

"You better get home," she says. "He says you took one of the lunatics."

"I didn't take her," I say. "She came of her own volition."

"Well, I'll just tell him that, then," she says sarcastically. "You'd better get on home."

"Fanny, I'm leaving with her," I say. "I need to come get some of my stuff." She is quiet; I am quiet. We listen to one another's breath for a moment.

"He ain't in right now," she says.

"I'll be over in a minute," I say. "I have got to go talk to some people."

"You are a fool," she says.

"I know," I say.

"How long you going for?"

"I don't know," I say.

"I'll make you some sandwiches," she says.

"Okay," I say. She hangs up. I say thanks to Fishly and go to the door, with the eyes of all of them on my back.

I stagger back toward the Eldo with my ruined finger held up high. The pounding in my joint is less violent when I hold it above my heart. I believe there is less blood getting to it when I hold it up there. One way or another, though, it hurts like hell.

I am not ready to deal with this latest turn of events. It seemed to me that things were complicated enough without Nigel's trying to blow the sheriff's poker party to smithereens on the eve of my departure; for I am positive it was Nigel, or at least that he had something to do with it. I am not sure that I take kindly to guerrilla acts that put my father at risk, even if I can join Nigel in suspecting the Doctor of foul play at one time or another, twenty years ago or a week ago.

I can only hope that no one has been inspired to link Virginia's escape and my absence with the bombing. Fishly had me worried for a minute there; but I let my imagination run away with me sometimes. No one, least of all Fishly, who knew me at the university as an apathetically drunken Deke, would suspect me of anything like that. I am about the least likely candidate there is for terrorist acts.

Do these latest events cause me to change my plans? I am a trifle overwhelmed by trying to work it out, swaying out there in the heat. As far as I can figure, the best plan for me is to proceed as I was going to, though the Doctor will probably not be in a mood to talk things out with me. He is likely out on a field trip with Hobson to track down the outlaws, or nursing a hangover in his office. I look down the block, to the pink-and-white awning that hangs limply in front of Candyland. The air buckles in the heat, my breath reeks, and my teeth ache, and I drag myself in that direction to get it from Daisy. That much, at least, will go as planned. She is sure to give me hell.

It turns out they are sitting right there in the front booth. Daisy's made-up face and the wide seersucker back of Mr. Brehard's coat face me. A roll of flesh swells from between the clean line of his short-cut dark hair and the fabric of his collar. It is not exactly muscle, but it is not fat either. It looks like a blood-sausage necklace. I am standing there dizzily staring at them when Daisy looks right into my eyes (or, rather, whatever it is that is reflected in the fly-eyed cop shades I am sporting) and pats her lips with her napkin and raises her eyebrows. She makes the motion of trying to swallow a big mouthful so that she can tell her father that I am in the window, but I open the door and go in before she can get it out.

He turns and surveys me. "You a little on the late side," he says.

"Yessir, I know," I say. "I had some pressing matters to attend to."

"Your finger," says Daisy.

"It got bit," I say.

"By a dog?" she says.

"No," I say. "It was a lunatic."

Mr. Brehard laughs. "Occupational hazard, heh-heh-heh," he says. I can see shreds of hamburger in his mouth.

"I can't work for you," I say. "I am going west to seek my fortune."

"You doing what?" he says.

"I am going to be a ceramicist," I say. "I hear that if you are going to make a name for yourself in that field, you have got to go west." Daisy dips a fry in ketchup and bites off half.

"Your daddy always said you were going to be a disappointment," he says.

"He is not wrong too often," I say. "Would you mind if I had a word with Daisy alone?" He is finished eating, anyway.

"Do ever what you please, son," Mr. Brehard says to me. "Have you talked to the Doctor about this? He was fixing to have a word or two with you today until he got about blowed up."

"I heard about that," I say. "No, I have not spoken with him yet. Do you think I should, Mr. Brehard?"

"I reckon any white man would," he says, sliding out of the booth. He puts a few bills from a slick alligator wallet on the table. "Does this mean you are not taking my daughter to the Neptune's Nuptials?" he asks.

"I am afraid so," I say. "But I know dozens of guys who are dying to take her." She drums her nails on the table, and he bends over and kisses her on the cheek.

"You tell me if you want me to have him killed when you get home, sweet thing," he says to her. He extends a meaty hand toward me. I hold up my finger apologetically and stick out my left, which he ignores. He reaches up and ruffles my hair like I am a kid. "I always thought you were a faggot, son, even when you were delivering papers for me way back when," he says, "but out of respect for your daddy and for your mother, may she rest in peace, I tried to make you feel at home. And when you started dating my Daisy, I said, well, at least he is one clever sumbitch even if he has got some faggoty leanings, which will probably make him nicer to her in the long run."

"I appreciate that, Mr. Brehard," I say.

"Good luck, son," he says, and heads for the door. We can see him start his car outside. He puts it into reverse, gives us a little wave, and turns his head over his shoulder and backs out of sight. He drove his car a measly half-block. I sit down, and Daisy pushes the fries my way.

"I feel sick," she says.

"I'm sorry," I say. "I know this is sudden."

"It's not you," she says. "Candyland always makes me feel sick."

"I'm sorry that happens," I say. "And I'm sorry I'm leaving."

"That's okay," she says. "I think Andrew Buford will take

me." Andrew Buford is a Deke who always insisted on giving me secret handshakes when we ran into each other. We have got the same thing tattooed on our ankles.

"That's good," I say.

"We've been getting to know each other a little bit," she says.

"Ah," I say.

"He's just so cute," she says, "you know?"

"I've always said so," I say.

"And you know," she says, dipping a fry, "he can flat go at it, too. Like a jackhammer."

And all this time I thought she wanted to marry me. Well, maybe she did. She just wanted to hump Andrew Buford some. Is that worse? I am not sure. I would like to think that I am a better humper than Andrew Buford, but I guess you can never tell. It might be that he is a dynamo.

"Well, tell him hi, will you?" I say.

"Sure," she says. "He really likes you, you know. He admires you."

"It's mutual," I say.

"Keep in touch now," she says.

"I will," I say, and I guess that is about it for me and Daisy. I hustle on out of there in a hurry.

My next stop is at the homestead. The live oaks of the drive spark in me the first pangs of premature nostalgia. Each sight, at this point, takes on the significance of a final vision: good-bye, oak trees; good-bye, white pillars; good-bye, green John

Deere tractor-mower; good-bye, home of my youth. Even the most committed and cowardly of deserters will be moved by doubt upon his final glance back at the encampment of his fellows, the watch fires smoking softly, the horses at tether, as he clambers over the rise into the woods and the unknown. The peace that pervades the atmosphere of the hospital belies the desperation of my flight and tempts me to linger.

Fanny is waiting for me at the kitchen table, with the blue vinyl picnic basket before her. She is drinking a cup of coffee. She sets it down and stands as I come into the kitchen.

"Hey, Fanny," I say.

"Hey, baby," she says, and takes me in an embrace, pinning my arms to my ribs. I cough from the pressure; I think she takes it for a stifled sob. "You going to be okay," she says.

"I know," I say. "I'm just not feeling too fit right now."

"You don't smell too good. You don't look too good, either. In fact, you look like you been run over," she says.

"That sounds about right," I say. "Look at this," I say, and hold out my finger.

"That's no good," she says.

"No," I concur.

"Well, sit down," she says. "Tell me what's going on."

"I can't," I say. "I need to get going."

"Just sit down for a minute, catch your breath, and have a cup of coffee. The Doctor is not around."

"Okay," I say. She pours me a cup of coffee. She is being unusually solicitous toward me, which makes me uncomfortable. I can only attribute her kindness to sadness at my leaving, and I would prefer we do not come to tears here; there is sure to be a flood if I crack.

The coffee is hot and strong, forcing a new surge of sweat out of my exhausted pores. I am vaguely embarrassed to be sitting here in so poor a state before Fanny.

"So what is it?" she says. "Why are you running off?"

"I'm in love," I say. "And it's time, anyway. I've got to make a fresh start."

"You are going about it ass-backward," she says, not without tenderness.

"I'm doing the best I can, Fanny," I say. "I don't mean to sneak off, but I'm not sure I can trust the Doctor. I wanted to talk to him, but I can't let him know where Virginia is at."

"He is mighty pissed," she says.

"I'm afraid of him," I say. "I have these ideas that he killed my mother. That he is responsible."

Fanny shakes her head. "It's your imagination, Billy," she says. "I told you before, don't nobody know what really happened."

"I think I know," I say.

"Well, there's no telling," she says, "but people will believe what they need to, and you can't stop them."

"I'm stuck on it," I say.

"There it is," she says, with finality. "I guess you'd best get your stuff before he comes back."

"Right," I say, and gulp my coffee.

Upstairs, the money is right there in the drawer with the stock certificate. I shove them both in my front pocket, and cast around the room for things I will need, and there is nothing there. I do not want any pictures or books, and those are the only things of value that I have in there. It is an empty feeling, to survey your past and find nothing that you want to bring with you into the future. I go back down the stairs and take my leave of Fanny. She is still at the table with the picnic basket.

"I'll miss you, Fanny," I say.

"I'll miss you, too, baby," she says. We embrace with the oddness of acquaintances at the moment of common loss: the taut synthetic feel of her uniform stretched across her back, the smell of lilacs and nylon and some kind of cleaning fluid. There is nothing else to say. I shoulder the bag and head out the door. On the way to the car I poke my head into the garage to see if there is anything I might want and remember a fishing rod of my maternal grandfather's that I never had the opportunity to use. It is a deep-sea rod.

I take its leather case from beneath the workbench and unbuckle it. The jointed rod is opalescent black, with loving patterns of shellacked thread wound at the bases of its eyelets. To its patinaed cork-covered base is screwed a reel of dusty green metal that is weighty with quality and spins on against the laws of physics when I flick the handle. The Doctor is not going to miss it. I will be able to use it, up to my hips in the surf of the Pacific. I have heard that the ocean there is colder than you would believe.

I replace the rod in its case and put it in the trunk of the car, with Fanny watching me from the porch. The trunk is so big that the rod case, the entire material of my future, looks lonely there, against the black nap of carpet lining.

" 'Bye," I say, and Fanny waves me off.

" 'Bye, Billy," she says.

"Fanny," it occurs to me to ask, "exactly where is the Doctor?"

"Oh, he's long gone out of town," she says. "He and that bastard Hobson gone out to your granddaddy's to get some dogs."

"No," I say.

"Oh, yeah," she says. "You ain't going to run into him."

I lay down some rubber on the way out, that is for sure, and then I am stopped as soon as I get going, by the frantically waving figure of Dr. Rosenthal, right at the gate. A herd of my lunatics stand around on the grass. "Hey, Billy," a few of them say, but most just stare off into space.

"Did you take her?" asks Dr. Rosenthal.

"You bet," I say, nudging the bumper forward against his knees. "Listen, I'm in a hurry, get out of the way," I say. He finally gives in, sidestepping and backpedaling, but then he reaches around the windshield and grabs my shirt. The pinions of his nostrils flare, like a hawk's stalling when it spots a rat.

"This is a legal matter," he says, "a serious legal matter. That woman was placed in the official custody of the state for a good reason: for the very good reason that she is ill. Very ill. I am calling the police."

"You do that," I say. "Just let go of me."

"I wash my hands of the matter," he says, and takes them off me to rub them against each other in symbolic cleansing.

I take the opportunity to ease away, honking apologetically at the patients who have wandered into my path, and when they disperse, I tear off.

On the highway to Peterson I pass the Doctor coming in the other direction. His car is maybe an eighth of a mile away when I realize, in a surge of panic, that it is he. Could it be that he has sniffed her out by this dumb chance, against all logic and probability, and even now has her bound in the back of his car? In his trunk? I freeze as his grille looms toward me in a geometric progression of size and speed. The time is too short between my realization and our passing for me to take any action, and in that instant we are side by side I note that his head is not even turned toward mine, but points straight ahead over grim fists, led by a cigarette clenched viciously between bared incisor bridges. He is in too much of a froth to notice that I am within five feet of him, and then I am gone. I watch the rearview mirror to see if he recognized me, if he is pulling off in a cloud of dust and bearing down on me in fell pursuit, but he does no such thing. The back of his fat sedan shrinks away into a curve. I saw no sign of Virginia in my father's vehicle, but I realize that in the doppler moment there was, in addition to the whine of engines and the rush of air displaced, a faint and stifled baying sound: the briefest snippet from the most mournful chorus in the world.

Circumstances are not so dire as I had feared. Things are pretty much the way I left them except that the hound dogs are gone from the run. Papa and Virginia have got some folding chairs leaned up against the shady side of the trailer. He has got a jar with him that from the look on his face I figure he has been working with for a while, and as I surmised, he has got her sucking on a fat plug. Rays of dark spit radiate from the twin foci of my lover and my grandfather. The chickens are keeping their distance.

"Oh, baby," I say, "I was afraid the Doctor got you." She shakes her head and shoots out a good stream.

"Papa hid me in the trailer," she says. "He is just the craftiest thing." She has not got the act of talking with a chaw in down yet, but it is kind of cute the way she wipes away the little bead that slips out the side of her mouth. Papa affirms her statement with a sage nod. His mouth is all caved in where his dentures ought to be.

"He come for the dogs," gums Papa, "though what the shit he hunting this time of year beats me."

"He is not hunting," I say.

"It beats the shit out of me," says Papa. I guess he did not hear me correctly. Varmints, the variety of species for which the hounds are bred and trained to hunt, are not in their prime in July. Most of them, due to the patchy quality of their coats, look like they have been nibbling on one another for most of the summer. You are supposed to hunt for them in the late fall and winter when their pelts are thick and shiny, though nobody I know bothers to tan them anyway these days. That kind of hunting is mostly just for the good time; you get drunk with some other boys and set your dogs loose in the woods and follow the noise they make until you find them howling under a tree some time near sun-rise, where you take turns with a police-issue .38 until somebody shoots the raccoon or weasel or what have you out of the tree. It is a big disappointment when it turns out to be a housecat, but I have only seen that happen one time.

"I say he ain't hunting," I say. "They are tracking down outlaws."

"It's as good a use as any, I reckon," says Papa.

"I guess so," I say. Papa takes a sip of his whiskey.

"I reckon you ain't got time to stay for a drink," he says.

"No," I say. "We need to get on the road before I falter in my resolve."

"I reckon you'd better," says Papa, and Virginia fishes out her chaw and stands up.

"We sure appreciate your help, Papa," she says.

"Yeah," I say. "Much obliged. Come and visit us."

"I reckon I might take one of them jet airplanes out there," he says. "I hear it is something special."

"Well," I say.

"Well," he says, and we hug. It is a real heartbreaker, and I do squeeze out a tear or two on the way out the drive. There is no point in denying your feelings.

So it looks to me as though my tenure in Tuscaloosa has come to an end. We are safe and on the road, with money, sandwiches, and a fishing rod. I figure the Doctor took the dogs back to the scene of the crime, so there will be little risk to stopping at Paradise to see if we can get that dope; and I would like to bid Nigel a final farewell, for what it is worth.

Virginia is beautiful. She is lit up with the glow of promise. Against all sense I have hope for our life together, and for the life of our child that is not yet born. It may be that I am a fool. It has been said before. Nevertheless, I am heady with the conviction that we can outrun the twin coursers, history and madness, that lope after us in the blue exhaust of the Eldo. They will be lost in the strange geography of a new land, baffled by the tall spires of the Rockies, desiccated by the deadly heat of the salt flats, drowned and broken under the gray walls of frozen water that beat against the coast from the north. The bend in my finger (it will never heal straight) will be the reminder of my commitment: desire and devotion made flesh, more permanent than any ring.

The singing of the bush is louder than ever, and the smells of growth and green decay hang under the leafy canopy. However, a peculiar quiet underlies the song of the garden and calls out its absence between the natural noises of the kudzu breathing and the animals calling; it is the absence of the funk of Paradise.

The clearing opens around us, in a great silence of sky. The pink hut stands as ever, a wisp of gray smoke rising out of its roof and losing itself in the cerulean vacuum above. Nigel sits on a pile of car tires, naked to the waist, wearing his shades, taking in the sun. He has an air of waiting: raises a slow palm in greeting as the Cadillac picks a path through the ruts in the clay over to where he sits.

"Back so soon," he says.

"Actually I'm leaving," I say. "I came to say good-bye. And maybe to get a bag for the road."

"You're going on a trip," he says.

"Yes," I say.

"Well, all right then," he says. "I believe I may be going on one myself."

"You had better hit it if you are going to," I say. "They are taking some dogs down to the station."

"I'm surprised they're not here yet," he says. "I hear it's a real mess down there."

"I heard that, too," I say.

"They'll be along soon," he says. "You had better do your business."

"Okay then," I say. "I've got three hundred dollars."

"That's pretty much money," he says.

"Have you got that much on hand?"

"No, I don't," he says. "I would say come back tomorrow, but there might not be one." He does not look too put out by the idea. I look around for signs of impending apocalypse, but there is nothing: just furrowed clay all around; fists of grass; cans and bottles; a hubcap, lying off to where the trees swell up; a cinder-block cube, painted pink; the bobwhites on the electrical lines.

"Don't talk like that," I say. "If you think they have got you, you can run off."

"I ain't going nowhere," he says, and takes a deep breath, and that is when the martins spew up out of the trace in a vortex of bright muscle, and a patrol car jounces out, followed by my father's. Nigel looks over at me.

"The shit is here, and you are in it," he says.

🍑

They bounce forward warily and take up a stand perhaps fifty feet away from us. I would tell Virginia to duck, but it is far too late. My father's car is in the corridor of shelter behind Hobson's; I see him step from it, out into the open, away from the car. The hounds thump metallically and wail from inside the coffin of his trunk, a curious sound track for this curious event. Hobson opens his door and gets out behind it, pistol in hand, leveled toward Nigel. Hobson looks behind, yells for my father to get back in his car, but the Doctor just puts his hands in his pockets and watches. Does his mind reel? I cannot tell from the set of his face or his posture. He looks no more than interested, a bystander.

"You all put your hands up!" yells Hobson. His voice is remarkably high for a man of his reputation. I have never liked the sound of it. A deputy opens the passenger door of the patrol car and points a shotgun in our direction. I put my hands up, and Virginia does the same, wiggling her fingertips. Nigel has raised his, as well, but he looks remarkably composed on his throne of rubber.

"Now, Billy, you and that girl step out of the car real slow and get out of the way, goddammit!" yells the sheriff, and we comply, keeping our hands raised, climbing over the doors of the convertible and stepping out of the line of fire. The Doctor begins a long stroll over to us, head down, his hands in his pockets. He is the only motion in the hole of quiet framed by the woods.

"Doc, you just cut that shit out," hollers Hobson. "Everbody hold real still." But the Doctor continues his stroll and comes over to stand beside me.

"Howdy, Nigel," he says, and, "Hey, Billy, Virginia."

Nigel does not look over.

"You can put them hands down, Son," says the Doctor to me. "You, too, young lady," he says. We bring them down slowly and try to figure where to put them. It is hard to remember where they normally go when someone has been telling you where to put them.

The deputy gets out of the car with the shotgun and walks over to Nigel in a crouch.

"Get up, boy," he says, and Nigel does.

"Now put your hands on that car there," he says. Nigel places his palms on the hood of the Cadillac, and the deputy frisks him with his left hand, holding the muzzle of the shotgun against the back of his skull with his right.

"He's clean, Sheriff," he says. They have been watching plenty of television to know how to talk like this.

"All right then, step away from him," says Hobson. "You keep your hands on the car, boy," he says to Nigel. He turns to me.

"Now what in the fuck is going on here?" he says.

"Nothing," I say. "There is nothing going on. Are you all here about the bombing?"

"That's right," he says. "What are you doing with this-here perpetrator?" He holsters his gun, leaving the snap open, and points meaningfully over at Nigel, as if to say, keep your damn hands on the hood. The deputy stands nervously at Nigel's back with the gun pointed at him.

"Hell, we were all right here when it happened," I say. "We were here from midnight till dawn."

"Doing what?" asks the sheriff. He has got a pinched-up weasel face. All the features are too close to the center of it.

"Well, sir, the truth is we were drinking, and we did smoke some marijuana, but we didn't blow nothing up. And Nigel was right here with us," I say.

"You all know him?" asks the sheriff.

"Yessir," I say. "I have known him since I was a baby."

"Is that a fact," he says.

"Yessir," I say.

"Do you know he is a nefarious goddamn criminal?"

"No sir," I say. "I mean, he might be one, but last night he was right here."

"How about you, young lady?" he says. "What you got to say for yourself?"

"Yes, that's right," Virginia says. "That's what happened." The Doctor looks at her with a strange little smile on his mouth.

"You the one this boy done busted out, ain't you," deduces Hobson, chuckling. I find it hard to fathom that the mood in the clearing is changing so fast. It is as if we are a wall of white that is so true and opaque in its whiteness, crazy or not, that it can blot out any fact.

"I busted out myself," she says.

"Well, I'll be," says Hobson. He crosses his arms, and

bends at the waist, in an avuncular, joking-probing fashion, to look us in the face, each in turn. I smell cigarettes on him, and a hangover that might match my own, and note the way his yellow upper teeth point down and in toward his gullet.

"You all are sure about this?" he says. We nod. "You be prepared to swear on it," he says.

"Yessir," I say. Hobson walks, just the way a sheriff ought to, over to where Nigel is sprawled against the hood.

"You one lucky nigger, son," he says. "I'll bet you know who done blowed up my office and some more, too. I got a mind to put them dogs on you right now." Nigel will not look at him. He just faces down into the white lake of the hood.

"I say you hear me?" says Hobson, and Nigel nods. Hobson goes on browbeating him, nigger this, nigger that, but you can see it is not going to come to anything. I am filled with wonder at what I have wrought.

The Doctor reaches over and slyly takes hold of my busted finger, squeezing it in a tight fist. I look down at our linked hands, which twist and shimmer at the bottom of a sea of pain. His fist is closed over my wounded digit in a squidlike stranglehold, the tendons popping and pulsing under his leathery skin as he grinds the bone fragments around in their meaty bag. I figure I am about to faint.

"I just want you to know that I am not buying this horseshit," he whispers.

"It's true," I creak.

"No, it ain't," he says. "In fact, I think you might even have tried to blow me up yourself."

"No," I say.

"It don't matter, one way or the other," he says. "I figure I am not going to see you again."

"No," I say.

"Love will make you forget yourself, I reckon," he says, his eyes roaming the skies.

"My finger hurts," I say.

"Yes," he says.

"I need to know some things," I say.

"What's that, Son?" says my father, giving an extra squeeze, almost of affection.

"I have been having these dreams, you know," I say.

"Yes," he says.

"I suspect that you are a bad man."

"Maybe so," he says. "I would like to think that these things are relative."

"No," I say.

"Well, you're young yet," he says. "In time you might understand."

"I will not," I say, but my voice breaks at the end there.

"We'll see," he says, and lets go. I figure that is the last time we will have any words between us and wonder if it is a good thing. I wonder if there is any getting out of your family. I wish I could bring myself to believe that you can, that my father is not as much inside me as my liver and kidneys and spleen, but there is no fooling yourself. I will never so much as look at the angle of my wrist when it lies loose, or turn to meet my passing profile in a shop window, without encountering him: not merely his shape, but the very structure of his most private self, mapped into the grid of my veins and the secret landscape of my retinas, and into the stutter and leap of my thoughts and dreams, as they coil themselves across synaptic chasms, under the black dome of my soul.

I surprise myself, and stay on my feet as he backs away toward the end of my tunnel of pain. Virginia is holding me up at the waist. Hobson gives Nigel a final cuff in the head, which dashes his face against the steel edge of the fender and knocks his shades to the ground.

The deputy is already back in the car, sitting there like he is waiting for a milkshake.

They drive off, and the last thing I hear from them is hound-dog yelps.

"That was close," I say. Nigel stands up from where he is spread out on the hood of the car, dabbing at the cut on his forehead. He is not bleeding too much, but getting hit like that has got to take it out of you.

"It was close, wasn't it, Virginia?" I say.

"Yeah, it was," she affirms, "but I think we'd better take a look at Nigel there. He got popped a good one."

"You're okay, aren't you?" I ask. He dabs away at the steady trickle of blood and looks around for his sunglasses. A rising exhilaration pools inside me as I realize the enormity of our victory; we have prevailed against the forces of evil in this little encounter at Paradise. I do not regret for an instant our having dropped by on the way out. It is more than fortuitous. It might be destiny. You can never tell when something is going to work out just right. "God, it is something," I declare. "We are all three of us free."

"It just makes me fucking sick," is all Nigel has to say about it. I am a trifle taken aback.

"What was it you were hoping for, there?" I ask. "It could not have gone much better if we had planned it."

"You're a big fucking hero," he says.

"That's not what I'm saying," I say. "I'm sorry you got hit in the head, but it is getting off pretty easy for terrorism and crimes against the state."

"I am not worried about my head," he says. He has come up with the sunglasses, which are twisted and dusty but unbroken. He bends them back and places them on his face with much care that the arms rest evenly above his temples and fit securely above his ears.

"Well, shit then," I say, "we are all of us okay." I am feeling expansive, despite his sour mood. "Nigel, you are like a brother to me," I say, and put an arm around him. What it is that I am feeling, I realize, is the thrill of having finally acted, and the beginnings of a synthesis of the complicated emotions I have always felt toward Nigel: fear, admiration, and the connection he has never acknowledged, the inevitable result of the circumstances we have in common.

"Shut up, Billy," he says.

"You have got to see this," I say.

"I'm not interested," he says, but in my excitement I am not to be stopped.

"It's like a motif," I begin. "You represent things to me.

You are strength, you are sexuality, you are danger!"

"Fuck you, Billy," he says.

"Oh no, man, I mean it," I say. "You are the coolest, and I am finally cool, too. I sent those fuckers back home!" I nod. It is all making sense. "We're intertwined, see, reflections of one another. I know it sounds funny, but it's true," I say. Nigel reaches an arm around my shoulder, as mine is around his. Some of his blood runs onto me. "Hey, that's kind of bad," I say. "You should put some raw meat on it or something."

"Never mind that shit," says Nigel. "I am fixing to tell you something."

"Anything," I say.

"You're going to hate it," he says.

"Okay," I say.

"I ain't no motif," he says, and pulls my face down and breaks it against the same edge of the fender that his got knocked against. "Ain't your brother. Ain't no mirror neither. Leave me out of that weird shit," he says, and does it again.

It is difficult to remember what being hit very hard feels like from one time to the next. The pain comes after the impact, which is a white vacuum of anticipation. My nose shatters on the steel, and my mouth fills with blood. There is blood all over the place. Nigel takes me by my armpits and helps me to the door of the Cadillac. Virginia climbs into the driver's seat. Nigel leans me over into the backseat and hoists me in by my belt. I am facedown on the leather in a slick of blood and spit.

Virginia asks him if he needs a ride anywhere, and he says

no thanks, and she drives away. I roll over onto my back, and the sky is obscured by the canopy of green, and we are rocking, rocking, and then we hit blacktop, and we are gone, really gone, and there is nothing for me to see but the darkening sky and Virginia's hair flipping around crazily in the wind of motion that buffets the car like a gale.

My mother found, to her delight, that the sky of the desert was altogether different from the skies she had known. She had always suspected that it would be so; she was well acquainted with stories about cowboys and sheikhs who spent all their lives under the sky of the desert, and who remarked often on the clarity and depth that were its particular magic. Indeed, the stars were brighter and more numerous even than she had imagined, and the sky behind them blacker. It seemed to her as though the fact of more stars, rather than brightening the sky, made the spaces between them more pronounced and mysterious. She became, in relation to the world, even smaller, but not in a manner that she found frightening or disturbing in the least. It felt to her as if her vision, which had been impaired for as long as she could remember, were finally restored. She saw that before she had only seen a cropped and filtered slice of the world, and that was why it had not made sense.

Carmen was the first to notice the light on the horizon. Both women were dreamy; at first they thought it was the sun come early, but then they remembered that the sun had set in front of them only a few hours before, and that it was

not likely to start rising in the west. Then they thought that
it might be a huge city, Houston maybe, though that was
on another road, whose lights were so fantastic that they set
fire to the sky above it. But then they saw that that, too,
was impossible, unless the city had been destroyed. Blades
of fire spread across the rim of the land like livid grasses,
seeding at the speed of sight. Phosphorescent mushrooms
sprang out of the flames and evaporated into the sky,
throwing off incandescent spores at the moment of dying.
An apocalyptic meadow was blooming over the desert.
There were no stars above it; they had been swallowed up
by the blackness between.

Their first instinct, once they were closer, was to turn
back. It was a fire on such a scale as might attend the
Second Coming: it was no meadow, but a jungle,
thousands of feet high, with trunks of fire towering and
buckling and ripping each other apart, and overhung with
oily smoke. When my mother and Carmen were within a
mile of it, they felt the heat slam against the front of the
car, and the air was poisoned with the stink.

"Lord, Carmen," cried my mother.

"I know, baby," said Carmen.

"He's behind us," she cried.

"I know, I know," said Carmen. "We got to keep on."
They could see the twin pricks of white behind them,
gaining on them, moving faster than they ever believed a
car could move, and they held each other hard and
proceeded directly into the fire. They were firm in their
intent. The last thing they saw in their rear window before
the flames engulfed them was the wild mouth of a man

with a hound's head, lips poised for a kiss.

It was incredibly hot in there. It had to have been; it was an oil fire gone crazy. I read that it covered five hundred square miles of the desert and melted the machinery of sixty-three wells. They shrank from the windows, which blackened and cracked, and their sweat sizzled and popped when it dripped from their bodies to the floor of the car, which shrieked and bubbled in the heat. To cool themselves, they sucked on the Nehis and rubbed the ice from the cooler across one another's skins. They thought it might never end, but in time the heat began to recede and the flames to shrink, and they rolled down the windows to take in the cold air blowing toward them from the mountains at the farthest reach of their sight, which were as sharp and white as the iguana's teeth.

*e p i l o g u e*

I DO NOT COME TO until we are under the arc lights of a gas station somewhere just inside Louisiana. My hands, run gently along the strange, damp curves, tell me that my face has come up like a fruit basket. My finger is still killing me where Virginia busted it. She is inside the glass room speaking to the station attendant, paying him out of my wallet. He bags two sodas and a pack of smokes and lays a sack of ice on the counter. It is gratifying to see that she is looking after me.

She does not know that I am watching her from the car. She looks like she could be any tired, pretty woman paying for gas. It might be that we are getting away.

I have got great hope, and a desperate thirst. Even now she steps toward me under the buzzing light.

# ABOUT THE AUTHOR

W. Glasgow Phillips grew up in Marin County, California. He received his B.A. in English from Brown University in 1992. This is his first novel.